Misfire
Life's Outtakes - Year 11

52 Humorous and Inspirational Short Stories

By
Daris Howard

A collection of stories, humorous anecdotes, thoughts, and tidbits of wisdom from the popular newspaper column.

Publishing Inspiration

Misfire

Life's Outtakes - Year 11

52 Humorous and Inspirational Short Stories

By

Daris W. Howard

A collection of stories, humorous anecdotes, thoughts, and tidbits of wisdom from the newspaper column *Life's Outtakes*.

ISBN-10: 1-62986-019-0
ISBN-13: 978-1-62986-019-0

www.publishinginspiration.com

Publishing Date: January 5, 2018

Publishing Inspiration LLC

Table of Contents

Dear Reader,

    People often ask me if my stories are true. Though I must admit that I tend to take a bit of literary license in my writing, each story is based on an actual event. Sometimes the stranger stories are the ones that are stretched the least. As people often say, truth is stranger than fiction.

    I also want to note that some of the names have been changed to protect the anonymity of the individuals.

Daris Howard

Finding New Meaning in Life

John had been going to the prison every week for six years to teach a Sunday School lesson to the men who wanted to attend. Every week for that whole six years, Dan had attended faithfully, dressed in a cowboy shirt, Levi's, cowboy boots, and a bolo tie. John was careful to never ask the men what they were incarcerated for, but he could see that Dan was a good man, and he just had to know. But it wasn't Dan he asked. He scheduled an appointment with the warden.

The warden welcomed John into his office and invited him to have a seat. When John mentioned Dan, the warden sighed.

"Dan's story is an interesting one. He was in his late twenties when he came here. He was convicted of petty theft, but the punishment was a life sentence, with twenty years minimum. It was fairly obvious the judge or someone had an ax to grind."

"How long has he been here?" John asked.

"Twenty-three years."

"So why doesn't the parole board free him?"

"I'm sure they would if he asked," the warden replied. "But Dan doesn't know what to do with his life now, so he doesn't ask. He's been here so long he doesn't think anyone would want him. He's a cowboy, and what little he stole was related to work, so he said he can't go back there."

John thought about it a lot, and the next week he visited with the warden again. "Can I take Dan on furlough for a day?" John asked.

The warden nodded. "Absolutely."

After the Sunday School class that week, John intercepted Dan as he was leaving. "Dan," John said, "I want you to attend church with me outside of the prison next week."

"Oh, no," Dan said. "I wouldn't know how to act or how to answer people when they ask about me."

"You'll be with me," John said. "I'll take care of it."

The next week, Dan came to Sunday School as usual, and afterward, though he was nervous, he walked out of the prison with John. When they arrived at the church, he was greeted as a friend. When people asked Dan where he lived, John simply gave them the name of the town where the prison was located. When they asked what Dan did, John answered that Dan worked in finance. After church, Dan went home with John's family and ate dinner. Then he sat in the big easy chair and read stories to the children. He seemed to enjoy that most of all.

When John took Dan back to the prison, they drove along silently. But when they arrived, John took Dan by the shoulder and looked into his eyes as he spoke. "Dan, there's a big world out there, with lots of good people. You have a good twenty years or more of your life to work. You could be a cowboy again, and maybe even have a family. Don't try to go back to where you were; go to a new state and start over." Dan didn't say anything; he just nodded.

The next week, when John started Sunday School, Dan wasn't there. He quickly learned that Dan had asked for and received parole. John learned pieces over the next few years as Dan sent short messages to the prison for him.

John found out that Dan had gone a couple of states away to apply for a job as a ranch foreman. The man who owned the ranch had died, and his wife was struggling to run it. Dan ran it well, and over time, the widow was able to look beyond Dan's past and fell in love with him. He helped raise her six children and became the most loving father and grandfather there ever was.

John enjoyed the brief messages he received. But his favorite was the last one.

"Thanks for helping me believe in myself. It is a big world out here, and there truly are a lot of good people."

John smiled and thought, "And Dan, you're one of them."

Member of a Band

My family was involved in a theatre production in an old theater. The men's changing room was nothing but an old converted closet. We were stuffed tight in there, which made for times of joking, telling stories, and barely getting into costume before the opening scene. One night we were still getting dressed when the pre-show started. I listened to one conversation with great interest.

David turned to Jim and asked, "Jim, did you sign up for a pre-show number? I heard you used to be in a band."

"Well, you might say that," Jim replied. "But some cows changed that."

"Cows?" David asked.

"I was in high school," Jim said. "There were four of us who decided we were really good musicians. We had big dreams of fame. The drummer's dad told us we could practice in his garage. But after about a week of practice, he changed his mind."

"So then what?" David asked.

"The lead guitarist lived on a farm with an old barn that was used for storing junk. It hadn't been cleaned since the cows had used it. The lead guitarist's dad said if we would clean and organize it, we could use it."

"That was nice of him," David said.

"I think he just wanted free labor," Jim replied. "Anyway, it took a couple weeks of working after school for us to get it clean. We were excited the day we moved in. We were a long way from anyone who could hear us, and we bragged about getting really good and then surprising everyone. We worked hard at it, too. We practiced every night. The problem was, we were all self-taught, and every practice was a bit different because we could barely read music. But the most annoying part of the whole thing was that when we practiced, the cows in the pastures would come to the barn and moo until we could hardly hear ourselves. Our keyboardist assured us that the cows just liked our music and wanted to join in."

"Did they?" David asked.

"I don't think so," Jim replied. "Once we thought we were really good, we started looking for gigs. We performed at a couple of places for free, but we were never invited back a second time. We finally got a non-paying gig at a bar, and we were paid in all of the Sprite we could drink since we were underage—too young for alcohol. No one cared what we played, and when the people got really drunk, they even tipped us a little bit.

"No matter what we did, we couldn't find any other place that would let us play. So then our drummer got this big idea. He said we should rent a big theater and invite everyone to come for free. He said we would pack the place and that would give us some recognition.

"We all agreed it was a good idea. The theater cost one thousand dollars for the night, so we each worked at part-time jobs to earn our shares plus a lot of extra for advertising. We rented the theater, made fliers, and posted them all over town. We put it on the marquee, bought ads in the paper, and did advertising everywhere else we could think of."

"How did it go?" David asked.

"When it was time for the concert to start," Jim replied, "not a single person had come, not even family and friends. So we opened all the doors and started to play, hoping to draw people in off the street. After about an hour, a lady and her daughter walked in and asked if they could sing. I said, 'Lady, can't you see we're having a concert?' She looked at the empty hall and said, 'It sounded so bad I thought it must be open mic night.'"

David laughed. "Ouch!"

"Yeah," Jim said. "Then the drummer said something which changed our lives forever."

"What?" David asked.

"He said, 'Guys, do you think that maybe all that time we practiced, the cows were really just begging us to quit?" Jim paused and grinned, then added, "And that's how I ended up in theatre instead."

Feeling My Age

I finished a goal that I wrote about in one of my stories ten years ago. The goal was to take each of my ten children on the hike to Table Mountain, which is just below the Tetons. I thought about the first time I took some of them up there, and I was already feeling past my prime then. But this time was even worse. And when I walked into church this last Sunday, someone asked me why I was limping. When I explained it was from blisters and told him why, he looked at me and said, "Hike that at your age? You're crazy!"

Maybe it was crazy. The hike is a grueling fourteen-mile round trip, climbing thousands of feet, some of it across granite and slippery shale rock. But the summit has a beautiful view. And I usually only have to make the hike once with each child. Then they usually decide they will never do it again.

But my youngest daughter turned thirteen recently, so I decided she was strong enough to make the climb. I had also never taken her sister, who is only two years older, so the three of us decided to make a day of it on the Saturday before Labor Day. I checked all my equipment the night before and found that my water purification pump had quit working since I last used it. That left no option but to carry extra water.

We got up at five o'clock and drove to the trailhead, arriving just before seven. We stretched, used the restroom, and headed on our way. The first part of the climb was quite strenuous, with switchbacks out of the parking lot up into the canyon. This soon turned into an easier upward trail.

The sun hadn't yet peered above the mountain rim when we reached the first-mile marker, and no one had passed us, so I felt we were doing really well. But as time went on, people started hurrying by. First just a few, then whole families. The extra water in my pack felt like it weighed a ton, and my muscles were shouting "Stupid!" at me with every step I took.

Once we reached the point where we felt too close to the summit to turn back, the trail turned steeply upward into switchbacks up the top of the canyon rim. I told my daughters it was time to cache more than half of the water and only carry what we would need to get us back to that point. My daughters readily agreed. We put the full water bottles into some brush and continued our climb. The higher we climbed, the more one daughter struggled with lack of oxygen. We started setting a goal of a hundred steps, then rest. A hundred steps, then rest. That later turned to seventy-five, then fifty, as the trail turned ever steeper.

More and more people passed us, but when a man who looked to be about eighty walked by, I began to question if I was delusional, especially since he was smiling. I have to admit that I was probably still the second oldest person on the mountain that day, but I doubted I would be making that hike twenty-five years from now. And I definitely would not be smiling if I did.

We made it to the top, had lunch, took pictures, and then turned to go back down. As I stood and my muscles screamed, I looked down and knew there was no other option. I warned my daughters that the hike down seemed to go forever, and indeed, I kept hearing, "Aren't we almost there yet?" more than I can count. But eventually, we made it.

For a reward, we stopped at a little drug store for ice cream. As we sat and ate, I said, "Well, my job is done. Now it'll be up to you to take your children up there."

My older daughter, wincing from the blisters on her feet, groaned. "When I get married, I think I'll move to a flat prairie and tell my children that mountains only exist in storybooks."

I smiled and considered that maybe I should have thought of that years ago.

Student Communications (2016)

Most of my college students are bright, fun to teach, and hard working. But each semester I get interesting letters, emails, phone calls, and other correspondence from a few students. I save these, and, occasionally, I compile them into a column. Over the last few years I have shared several of these, and with school just starting, I thought I'd share a few more. I don't think any of these comments need any explanation other than to say that I changed or removed any names for anonymity. Also, I pared a few of them down a bit.

*****

Email Correspondence

Girl: Did someone by chance happen to turn in a phone to you after class today (Monday)? It's an iPhone 6, and it's a rose-gold color.
Me: Yes. I have it in my office.
Girl: Awesome! Thank you! Will you be able to bring it to class on Wednesday?
Me: Yes. Can you live without it that long?
Girl: Haha! Yes, I'll be fine. It's too much of a distraction anyway. I do better in my classes without it. I ought to just get rid of it.

*****

Dear Professor Howard, I wanted to write to tell you how much I enjoy your class. I have never been good at math and have always struggled to get the concepts. With the humorous scenarios and stories you tell to help us understand the concepts, the class is a lot more fun. I still don't get the math, but at least I'm enjoying the class while I'm not learning the math.

*****

Professor Howard, I am really mad. You said the test was right out of the homework, but the problems had numbers changed in them, and I had all of the homework answers memorized.

*****

Professor Howard, I am really ticked off about the test, especially problem twelve. I don't think it was fair. I know we went over it the day of the test review, but I didn't understand it, and I don't think it's fair to put something on the test that I don't understand.

*****

Hi, Professor Howard. In class today you said that the average on the test was over 80%. I think that I must have gotten the wrong exam when I went to the testing center because I really bombed it and was nowhere near 80%. I got into the testing center yesterday, and yes, it was over polynomials and the things that we did in class, but I couldn't figure out a single problem. It was like nothing I remember doing. So what I'm thinking is that maybe I got some other teacher's test and not yours. It did have your name at the top as the teacher, but I think maybe the computer did that by mistake, too, because as little as I knew I'm sure it couldn't be the right test. Is there a way I could be given a chance to retake it so I can get the right exam?

(I let him retake it just to see if something was wrong and then got this note.)

Professor Howard, I went in to take the test again, and it was the same test, and I didn't understand it any more than I did before. Maybe I should come see you for some help.

*****

Hi, Brother Howard. You know that project quiz that had one true/false question. I did it and got it wrong. I was wondering if there was any way you would reopen it for me because I'm sure I know the right answer.

(I wrote her back and said that if she would show me her work, I might give her partial credit, and she said no, it was okay. She thought she would skip it.)

*****

Dear Teacher, Is it possible that I could turn the assignment in another day? I have had a relapse with my cold/flu, and I am having a hard time constipating, but I will get it done.

Practice and Performance

I was an offensive guard on my high school football team. We had a good line, and we worked hard and practiced hard. Our running backs were incredibly talented, but too often, because of their talent, they didn't practice to their full potential. Johnson, our leading receiver, was the worst. He would run down field, turn, and catch just about anything the quarterback threw at him. He would almost always catch the passes, but he was often sloppy. He and I were two opposites. What I lacked in talent I made up for in intensity, and many of the other players yelled at me for it.

Our first game was coming up, and our coach wanted us to practice as if we were in a game situation. The offense huddled, and the quarterback called a pass to Johnson. We lined up, and the ball was quickly snapped. The line defended well, and Johnson caught the pass and slipped past the defender. He ran a short distance, and then Johnson and the defender stopped and walked back to the scrimmage line.

Coach turned to the defender. "Hazelton, why did you stop?"

"Johnson caught the ball," Hazelton said.

"But he was still seventy yards from the goal line!" Coach yelled. "Do you plan to just let the receiver waddle down for a score in a real game?"

"No," Hazelton said meekly.

Coach then turned to Johnson. "And Johnson, what was that little dance you did after you caught the ball? Why didn't you run for the goal?"

"It's just practice, Coach," Johnson said. "No need to wear ourselves out."

Coach was livid. "Well, you better wear yourself out. The linemen are going full force, and you better be, too."

A couple of running plays were called and then another pass. Johnson caught the ball and did his dance again, then he and the defender came walking back. Coach could take no more.

Coach yelled to the quarterback, "I will decide what plays you call from now on." Then he turned to me. "Howard, you are defensive tackle."

"But Coach," I said, "I've never played defense before."

"You know what the line does," Coach replied. "And all you have to do is get whoever's got the ball. Just go after them with the same ferocity you use to defend on offense."

I nodded and moved into the defensive tackle position. The ball was snapped, and the fullback came through the line carrying the ball. I tackled him at the line of scrimmage.

"Howard," he yelled, "don't hit so hard. It's just practice."

The next play was a pass, but before the quarterback got it off, I tackled him. "Criminy, Howard," he said. "It's just practice."

The next play was another pass. This time, the quarterback quickly got it off, and Johnson evaded the defender and caught it. I was already headed toward that part of the field. Johnson did his little dance and turned just as I hit him. As I stood and helped him to his feet, he started yelling and swearing at me. "It's just practice, you idiot."

I jogged back to the line, and Johnson walked. The whole way there I could hear him swearing at me even while Coach was praising me.

Coach called another pass on the next play. Again, the quarterback got it off quickly, and Johnson caught it. But this time he looked and saw me coming. He turned and ran. We ran the whole length of the field, and even though he was slightly faster, he apparently thought I would quit and turn back, so he slowed. I tackled him only a few yards from the goal line. If he had been mad on the previous play, it was nothing compared to this time.

When he approached the line, still swearing at me, Coach told him to shut up. Coach then turned to me. "Howard, tell everyone what you told me when I asked why you're so intense."

"You perform like you practice," I replied.

Coach nodded and turned to the rest of the team. "You all remember that. You perform like you practice."

The Dating Coach

The guys I hung out with were all gathered around the cafeteria table eating lunch when the conversation turned to girls. Rod began bragging about how great he was at picking up girls. He went on and on about how he was so smooth that there wasn't a girl that could withstand his charm.

"I don't know," Lenny said. "A girl would have to be desperate to go out with you."

"Very funny," Rod said. "The thing is, I know that girls think differently than we do."

"Thank you, Einstein," Lenny said sarcastically. "The last time I took a girl out I asked her what she wanted to do, and she said, 'surprise me.' I guess she actually didn't like surprises because she never went out with me again."

"What did you take her to?" Rod asked.

"A tractor-pulling contest," Lenny replied.

Rod rolled his eyes, while I found myself thinking about how much I liked tractor pulling contests and wondered what the problem was.

"If a girl goes out with you," Rod said, "she's expecting something romantic, something that focuses on her."

Dennis, the only other boy in our group besides me who had never been on a date, was listening intently. Dennis had big glasses and was one of the school nerds. "But how can you do something a girl would like to do if you can't get one to go out with you?" he asked.

Rod looked at Dennis with pity, and then an excited grin broke across his face. "Hey, Dennis," he said. "I've got an idea. Why don't I become your dating coach? We'll prove to everyone how great I am."

"This should be good," Lenny smirked.

Rod ignored Lenny and focused on Dennis. "Let's start right after lunch. The first thing we need to do is build you up a bit. We'll go lift weights."

I lifted weights during lunch hour, so I was there when Rod and Dennis came in.

"I've never lifted weights before," Dennis said.

"There's nothing to it," Rod replied as he set up the bench press at about a hundred pounds.

Dennis couldn't budge it, so Rod kept taking weight off until it was at fifty pounds. Sweating and grunting, Dennis raised it about an inch. A little less weight and Dennis finally made the ten repetitions that Rod wanted. When he finished, Dennis looked like he was only a few steps away from death. Rod pushed Dennis hard and got him through most of the different stations before the bell rang.

As they walked out the door, Dennis spoke with great disgust. "I'm sweaty, and I smell terrible."

"That's attractive to girls," Rod said. "Remember, I told you they think differently."

"Wow!" Dennis said with surprise. "That's really weird."

Lenny had joined us in the weight-room, and he said, "Yeah, girls are weird. Almost as weird as Rod."

The next day, Dennis waddled into first-hour class, groaning all the way to his seat.

"How's it going?" Lenny said as he grinned and slapped Dennis on the back.

Dennis yelped in pain. "Rod, are you sure this will work?"

"Of course," Rod said. "Don't worry, we've only begun."

I grinned when I heard Dennis sigh and mumble, "Maybe it'd be better if I just stayed single."

The Dating Coach 2

Rod considered himself the best ladies' man in the high school, and he decided to prove it. He claimed he could turn Dennis, the school nerd, into a social Do
n Juan. Lenny was foremost to express his doubt, but we were all interested in the experiment.

First, Rod got Dennis to lift weights. He convinced Dennis that he needed muscles and that girls liked the smell of sweat. We had our reservations, but after a couple of weeks of waddling sorely into class, Dennis's physique did seem to be changing slightly.

"Hey, Dennis," Lenny said, "is there actually a muscle where your biceps are, or is that just a nasty pimple?"

Dennis grinned. "I've gone from benching thirty pounds clear up to fifty. See?" With that, he flexed his biceps.

Lenny slapped Dennis on the back. "You're right. It *is* slightly bigger than a pimple."

I had to admit that Rod's coaching seemed to be working. With the added muscle, Dennis was also gaining confidence, and the confidence was more important than the muscle.

Rod decided it was time to work on Dennis's conversation skills. "Okay, Dennis," Rod said. "Let's pretend that I'm a girl and you want to talk to me. What are you going to say?"

Lenny spoke before Dennis could. "I'd say you are one ugly girl."

"Buzz off," Rod said. He then turned back to Dennis. "Okay, Dennis, give it a try."

Dennis thought for a moment and then smiled. "What do you think about the quadratic formula in algebra? Pretty cool, huh?"

Most of the guys rolled their eyes, and Rod just shook his head.

"Look, Dennis," Rod said, "you've got to talk about what the girl is interested in."

"But I don't know what girls are interested in," Dennis replied.

"Then just do this. Let her do the talking, and you just agree with her. Let's try it. Okay, so pretend I'm the girl, and I say, 'It's a beautiful night for a walk.'"

"But it's supposed to rain tonight," Dennis said.

Rod breathed a big sigh. "It doesn't really matter, Dennis. Just agree with her."

They practiced again, with Rod saying something and Dennis agreeing. As they continued to practice, Lenny sidled up to me. "I'll bet you your dessert from lunch that this is going to end badly. Girls never think or say what you expect them to."

I had to agree, but I couldn't help but take the bet, especially as I watched Dennis pour his whole heart into his training.

Rod continued to have Dennis lift weights and practice the phrase and agreement process at every lunch hour. We were all ready to see Dennis make his attempt, but Rod wasn't taking any chances. He planned to try out every phrase he thought a girl might say and make sure Dennis's responses were perfect. Finally, after a couple weeks of practice, Rod could think of no new phrases, and Dennis was hitting the ones thrown at him spot on. I was even beginning to think I might win Lenny's dessert.

The big day finally arrived, and Rod made sure Dennis's hair and clothes were aligned. Dennis walked across the cafeteria to Missy, the girl he hoped to ask on a date. The rest of us tried to act like we were nonchalantly eating as we watched. It all seemed to be going well for Dennis, and he and Missy were even eating lunch together. Rod was grinning, sure of his success, when Missy suddenly slapped Dennis, knocking his glasses off and making him drop his lunch tray. Janitors scurried to clean up the mess, and Dennis hurried back to our table.

"What happened?" Rod demanded.

"Well, I agreed with her on everything like you taught me. But then she said something we hadn't practiced."

"Did you agree with her on it?" Rod asked.

"Yes," Dennis replied.

"What did she say?" I asked, reluctantly handing Lenny my cinnamon roll.

"She said, 'I think these school lunches are making me fat.'"

Bear Scare

Rick and his family planned one last campout before winter. It was still warm, but the crisp evening air warned that winter storms were drawing near. So they hitched up their camper and drove to the woods, enjoying the fall colors.

They checked into the campground and set up camp. They ate a delicious meal, and then Rick went to visit his neighbors. He liked to meet people from other places, and a campground usually included travelers from many locations. All the other campers were pleasant except for one couple who made it clear that they weren't interested in visiting with Rick. The wife was especially terse and let him know that she wanted him to leave.

Rick returned to his camp, and he and his family sat around the campfire watching the flame flicker as they visited and told stories. They ate some last-of-the-season watermelon and even had a seed spitting contest. Before it got dark, Rick led all of his children to the outhouse so they wouldn't have to make the trip later. As he sat down to use the facilities, he noticed a sign posted on the bathroom door, impossible for the captive audience to miss.

"You are in bear country. Make plenty of noise when you go into the woods. If you are moving around the campsite at night, especially coming to or from the outhouse, make lots of noise to avoid surprising any bears."

Rick had been camping a lot, and he knew that surprised bears are not friendly bears. He returned to camp still thinking about the interesting sign.

Before they retired to bed, Rick's family looked at the beautiful, starlit sky. They had a final bedtime snack of milk and cookies, and then everyone was tucked into bed.

Rick didn't know how long he slept, but he was suddenly very uncomfortable. He quickly realized that he had eaten far too much watermelon in order to win the seed spitting contest. He didn't relish the thought of getting out of his nice, warm bed and traipsing out into the cool fall air, but he knew he would have to sooner or later, and he wouldn't sleep until he did.

He slipped his feet out of bed and slid them into his sandals. He pulled on a robe, grabbed a flashlight, and quietly left the trailer. He shivered as he made his way to the bathroom, not even thinking about the bear warning sign. But once he sat down, there it was, big and bold. He smiled to himself. He was not about to wake the whole camp making noise. His flashlight should be sufficient to scare any bear.

He finished and stepped outside, only to hear a sound some distance away. He instantly thought "bear," but then he laughed to himself. Bears don't bang spoons against pans. He could see a light coming toward him from the campsite of the unfriendly people. He left his own light off and watched as the other light grew closer. The person had a flashlight and a spoon in one hand and a pan in the other and was banging the spoon against the pan loud enough to wake the entire camp.

Rick moved into some bushes near the outhouse and watched. He knew what he wanted to do, but should he? Could he ever forgive himself if he did? Would he always regret it if he didn't? As the person came closer, he could hear a woman's voice shivering, likely more from fear than from cold. "Go away, bear. I'm here and don't want to surprise you, so go away."

Rick knew he would never forgive himself, but he just couldn't pass up this opportunity. Just as the lady was right across from him, he let out the deepest, loudest roar he could. The lady let out a scream, dropped the pan, and ran a record forty-yard dash back to her trailer. She banged on the door with one hand as she faltered to open it with the other.

The next morning Rick smiled innocently when the ranger came around to warn everyone about a reported bear encounter the night before. Rick held out the pan.

"While you're at it," he said, "you might ask if anyone lost this last night."

A Crusty Fall Freeze: Barnyard Humor

It was late October, and Butch and Buster, my two friends, had come to visit after school. They weren't farm boys. They had grown up in the backwoods of a state further east, so when it came to cattle, they might as well have grown up in the city. They did like to come out to the farm, but it almost always ended up turning into a dare session between them.

That October we'd already had a couple of cold nights, well below freezing, and Butch and Buster joined me to check the cows. The cows were mooing, usually a sign that they are out of water, and just as I figured, the watering trough had a slight crust of ice over it.

While I was looking for something I could use to break the ice, Buster stared intently at the corral. Eventually, he walked over to a flat, frozen cow pie.

"Hey, Butch," Buster said, picking up the cow pie. "Look at this cool toy disk."

"That's not a toy disk," I said. "It's a frozen cow pie."

"What's a cow pie?" Buster asked.

"Cow poop," I replied. "Also known as cow chips, ordure, or meadow muffins."

Butch started to laugh. "Buster is playing with cow poop. He's the cow poop man."

"Well, it looks like a toy disk," Buster said. "And I bet I can cow poop you upside the head with it."

Buster immediately let it fly in Butch's direction and barely missed hitting his brother.

"Oh, yeah?" Butch said. "I can throw better than you."

Butch picked up a frozen cow pie and flung it in Buster's direction. It fell far short, and Buster jumped up and down, laughing.

"You can't even throw it far enough. You're Butch, loser of the Olympic cow chip toss."

Soon frozen cow pies were flying back and forth almost as fast as insults. Meanwhile, I was hunting for something to break the ice, glad I wasn't in the middle of their competition.

"Hey, guys, I need to go find an ax to break this ice," I said. They paused their chipathon, so I pointed at a large brown mound about thirty feet across. "My dad told me to make sure that you don't walk across the manure pit."

"What's a manure pit?" Butch asked.

"It's where the wet manure flows out of the barn," I replied. "Usually it's wet, but it's frozen over."

I left to get the ax, and when I returned, I was shocked to find both of them standing a few feet from each other over the center of the manure pit. Of course, when I say I was shocked, I mean I would have been if it had been anyone besides Butch and Buster.

"What are you doing out there?" I yelled.

"Buster dared me," Butch said. "He said I didn't have the guts to cross it."

"And Butch said he was braver than me and could cross first," Buster added.

"Well, get off of there," I said.

"We can't," Buster replied. "Every time we move, we can hear it crack."

"I'll get a board," I replied.

I found a long two-by-six and carefully pushed it across the crust toward them. It reached within a couple of feet of them. At almost the same instant, they both yelled, "Me first!" and stepped toward the board. Suddenly, the crust gave way, and they both disappeared. My heart pounded until they reappeared, sputtering and shivering.

"Grab the board," I yelled. They did, and I pulled them out. "My dad's going to kill me," I said, rushing them to the house to get them cleaned up and some clean clothes.

Looking at their ruined clothes, Buster said, "I don't think our dad's going to be thrilled."

That night my dad asked what had happened, and I told him the story. "Well," he said, "you should know that when I tell you to keep them from doing something, the last thing you want to do is tell them not to do it—because then they will." He laughed. "But I guess they learned their lesson, because their dad said that when they got home, their old granny scrubbed them until they were all pooped out."

An Honest Thief

As I read about all of the refugees in the world right now—an estimated sixty million, with half of them children—my mind returned to this time of year when I was twenty years old living in New York. I was doing missionary work with three other young men, and the holidays were approaching. Times were tough. The GM plant, the biggest employer, had shut down, and a lot of people were thrown out of work. In some areas, the crime rate was spiraling out of control as otherwise good people turned to theft. As missionaries, we spent lots of time finding needy families and making sure they had food and possibly a few simple toys for their children, helped by donations from church relief efforts.

As we spent lots of time in this work, I was usually too busy to think of anything else, but as I climbed into bed at night, my thoughts turned to home. My family, though not wealthy, would have a bounteous harvest from our garden and farm. In my teenage years, my mother would have me deliver plates of holiday cookies and candies to widows and needy families.

In this mix of thoughts and events, something interesting happened. As we were finishing up one evening, one of the other missionaries, Johnson, realized he had left his wallet on the front seat of our car. Knowing the car and the garage were both locked, he decided he wouldn't worry about going out in the cold to get it.

The next morning, we had breakfast and prepared for our day's work. Johnson unlocked the garage, and I opened the overhead door while the others went to the car. Johnson unlocked the car, climbed in, and gasped.

"Howard," he said, you've got to see this."

Johnson's wallet lay open on the seat of the car, and beside it was a note. I picked it up and read it.

I'm sorry that I had to take money from your wallet. I lost my job, and I haven't been able to find any other work. My wife left me, I had nothing to buy milk with, and my baby daughter was hungry. I'm not a thief, and I promise I will pay you back. I hope that since you're men doing God's work, you will understand and will forgive me.

"That's all the money I had until the end of the month," Johnson complained. "Now what will I do?"

"He said he'd pay it back," Stanton, another missionary, said.

"Yeah, right," Johnson said. "Like that's really going to happen."

"How much was it?" I asked.

"Five dollars," Johnson replied.

"Isn't that what we're doing out here anyway?" I asked. "I mean, if he needed it, wouldn't you have given it to him?"

"I suppose," he replied. "But I don't like the idea of someone just stealing it."

I opened my wallet and handed him a ten-dollar bill. "I've bought enough groceries to last me a while. You take this."

"Do you have any more to last you through the rest of the month?" Johnson asked.

"No," I replied, "but my bills are all paid. I'll be fine."

He reluctantly took it because he needed it, and we left for work.

After a couple of weeks, we had pretty much forgotten about the incident. Then one morning we felt a sense of déjà vu. We opened the locked garage, opened the locked car, and there on the seat was a five-dollar bill with a note. It said, "Thanks for the loan. I got another job."

Davis, another one of the missionaries, said, "Have you considered what kind of man has the skill to break into a locked garage and a locked car, steal money, and then pay it back?"

"Yes," I said, smiling as they handed me the five dollars. "It's the kind of man who is a good man and loves his daughter."

The Halloween Surprise

While I was visiting with my friend Tim and his wife, Sally, I asked them how they met. Tim looked at Sally, and an embarrassed grin spread across his face.

"Maybe I should let Sally tell the story," he said.

Sally laughed. "I'd be happy to. You see, when we were in high school, Tim and my twin brother, David, were best friends. The problem is, I kind of liked Tim, but he didn't even know I existed."

"That's not totally true," Tim said. "I knew you were David's sister. I'll admit I didn't pay much attention beyond that, but I did know you were his sister."

"Did you even know my name?" Sally asked.

Tim shrugged. "I didn't need to. I just called you 'David's sister.'"

"Anyway," Sally continued, "a Halloween party was coming up, and I really wanted to go, especially since I knew Tim would be there. I asked David if he could give me a ride, and he told me he was going with Tim. I begged to go, and he finally said it would be okay if I didn't bug them or say anything. So, to be funny, I decided to go as a mime so I couldn't say anything.

"Halloween was on a Saturday that year. Tim was scheduled to pick David up at about six. But earlier in the day, David came down with a bad case of the flu and could hardly get out of bed. I didn't know if I'd still be able to go to the party or not. And not only that, David told me he'd forgotten to ask Tim if I could catch a ride. David said he was too sick to call Tim and cancel, so he suggested I just ask Tim for a ride when he came."

"But she didn't," Tim interjected.

"I'm getting there," Sally said. "Tim didn't know I was going, and since he also didn't realize David wasn't, I decided to have a little fun. I stuffed my shoulders and tried to make myself look as masculine as I could. I also really put on the mime paint to hide my looks. When Tim came, I went out to the car, and when he said something to me, I signaled that I was a mime."

"Yeah," Tim chimed in, "and she totally pretended she was David."

"I was a bit annoyed that Tim couldn't tell I was a girl," Sally said. "Even as much as I worked to look like a boy, I still expected he would eventually realize who I was. But he never did. And then, all night, all he talked about was how annoying girls were. Oh, he would talk a little about this cute girl or that cute girl, but mostly he just said they were annoying."

"And to make matters worse," Tim added, "still pretending she was David, she used hand gestures to ask what I thought of his sister."

"And after he talked all about how annoying I was," Sally said, "I felt like slapping his face. But instead, I just ignored him the rest of the night."

"And I couldn't figure out what was wrong with David," Tim said. "Obviously, he wasn't going to speak to me if he was a mime, but I was sure he was giving me the cold shoulder. I took Sally home, still thinking she was David, and she got out, slammed the car door, and went into the house. I didn't figure it all out until the next day when David thanked me for giving Sally a ride to the party."

"Then what did you do?" I asked.

"He brought me some flowers and an apology note for being such a jerk," Sally replied.

"And when I handed them to her," Tim said, "I suddenly realized how pretty she was, and it all moved forward from there."

"Yes," Sally said. "But when I'm mad at him, I just dress up as a mime so he'll get it."

Tim laughed. "Yes, and that's when I know I need to get some flowers and apologize."

The Christmas Gift

My son Scott and his wife, Janalyn, lived with us for a while this summer after their graduation from college. His job didn't start until September, and it gave us a chance to get to know Janalyn. Our life is quite a bit different from how she grew up. She had never canned food before, and she soon learned the joy of home-canned fruits, vegetables, jams, and jellies. We told her that whatever she picked from our big garden, she could can, and we would even provide the bottles. While Scott worked to make some money for their move, Janalyn worked hard, canning dozens of jars of jam and fruit. By the time they packed the truck to start their new life in New York City, they had lots of delicious homegrown food to take with them.

When we asked them what they wanted for Christmas, it was no surprise that Janalyn said she wanted a pressure canner of her own. We knew we couldn't afford a new one of the quality we wanted for her, so we started looking for a nice used one. But she found one before we did. It was almost new and was about half price. The problem was that they had no car, and it was a couple hours away by light rail and train.

Scott, wanting to buy the canner for his wife's Christmas present for, got off work a little early Friday evening and boarded the light rail. After a couple of transfers, he rode the train for the final leg of the trip. True to his word, the man selling the canner was waiting. Scott bought the canner, looked at the train schedule, and found out he had an hour and a half before the return train would arrive. The station was closed, so he set the canner on the ground, leaned against it, and started reading a book. It wasn't too long before he heard a sharp, commanding voice. He looked up and saw two police officers with guns drawn standing at opposite sides of him, each about fifty feet away.

The officer spoke again. "Step away from the canner."

Suddenly, Scott thought about the Boston Marathon bombing and realized what this Christmas gift looked like. He stood and did as he was told. After checking his identification, one of the officers, who knew a little bit about canning, asked Scott some questions. Finally, satisfied that Scott had bought the canner for the purpose he claimed, the officers allowed Scott to open his canner so the officers could see it was empty.

By this time, a third officer had shown up, and not long after that, the police commander arrived. This was more excitement than their little town had had in a while. Once everyone was satisfied that Scott was harmless, one of the officers informed him they also had the K-9 unit and the bomb squad ready and waiting not far away. The first officer apologized to Scott and explained that their town had lost fourteen people in the 9/11 attack on the World Trade Center.

"Everyone is really vigilant now," the officer said.

Scott said he didn't mind. In fact, he was happy they were so careful. The first two officers stayed with him until the train came. They even informed the conductor that Scott and his canner were okay. But Scott found that as he traveled, even though he left the lid off so everyone could see the canner was empty, no one trusted him. He sat at the back of the train and the light rail, and as people came back and saw the canner, they immediately went back to the front. Soon, no matter what he was riding, he had the whole back end to himself while the front was packed tight. He felt bad, and he understood how they felt, but he still had to get the canner home.

Eventually, he arrived at their little apartment, and Janalyn was there to greet him with a hug. He told her the story.

As he finished, he said, "I'm glad you like to can. But if we ever need a new pressure canner, maybe next time we'll just order it on Amazon and have it delivered."

When to Keep Your Mouth Shut

Cyrus was an old farmer and had worked hard all his life. He was independent, but he was getting older, and everything was just a little bit harder. Still, he was determined to maintain his independence and pride.

When the Boy Scouts came around wanting to rake his leaves, he shooed them away, telling them he was capable of doing his own yard work. When he hurt his back, the men of the community wanted to help him stack his wood, but Cyrus wouldn't hear of it. Even if he could only carry one small stick of wood at a time, he was determined to do it himself.

One fall day, there was a big agriculture expo at the local university. Though Cyrus was retired from farming, the monotony was driving him crazy, so he decided to go.

"Take some food with you," his wife said as he was heading out the door. "You know how you get at those farm things, staying for hours. And since you get dizzy when you don't eat for a long time, you'll need something."

Cyrus didn't like the implication that he was old and feeble. He only pretended to take something, and then he slipped out and was on his way. Once at the expo, Cyrus was in the world he loved. He knew half the people walking around the big football field where the agriculture exhibits were displayed. New tractors, combines, hay equipment, and tillage machines were there.

The time went by quickly, and Cyrus realized he had that dizzy, low-blood-sugar feeling. He decided to visit one of the food booths. But they were on the far end of the football field, and there were a lot of things to stop and look at on his way.

He was getting close to the hamburger stand he was aiming for when suddenly, everything went black. When Cyrus came to, he was lying on the artificial turf with paramedics leaning over him. No matter how much Cyrus complained, they insisted he had to go to the hospital just to be safe. That made Cyrus mad, but he didn't have much choice. When he finally got to the hospital, they checked him over and felt he was okay to go home.

As he was reaching for the phone to call his wife, he was so mad that he mumbled, "I think I'm going to go home and shoot myself."

He, of course, didn't mean it, but the hospital staff was trained to take suicidal threats seriously. So they took him, hollering, back into the hospital. He was informed that they legally had to watch him for forty-eight hours.

If he was mad before, it was nothing compared to his attitude now. He called his wife, and she hurried over. But he still had to stay for the full two days. He was upset, and for forty-eight hours he made everyone's lives miserable until they were as happy for him to leave as he was. When his release day finally arrived, he was about to march out when the hospital staff informed him that hospital policy required them to wheel him out in a wheelchair.

That was the last straw. He stormed out before they could stop him. But just after he stepped outside, he slipped on the newly snow-covered sidewalk, fell, and broke his hip. Back into the hospital he went, riding not in a wheelchair, but on a gurney. This time he stayed a couple of weeks. When he was finally released, he humbly accepted the wheelchair ride.

As his wife walked beside him, she asked, "Cyrus, have you learned anything from all of this?"

"Yes," Cyrus replied. "I have learned that there's a time to keep my mouth shut."

A Thankful Attitude

Two girls sat next to each other on the first day of my class. They didn't know each other, and their differences were stark. Melanie was drop-dead gorgeous. She had blond hair and blue eyes, her hair was styled perfectly, and her clothes were the latest style, indicating she had plenty of money. Alana was quite plain-looking with dark hair and brown eyes. Her hair was pulled back into a cute braid, and her clothes, though neat and well taken care of, were not the latest style, and it was easy to see that her family had to be careful with their finances.

But the most notable physical difference of all was that Alana had been born without forearms. Her hands were where most people's elbows would be. During the first day of class, I watched the two girls. Melanie wrote easily, taking notes quickly. Meanwhile, Alana struggled. She had to bend close to her paper to write because of her shortened arms.

Over time, I noticed that almost everything was harder for Alana than it was for Melanie. Not only was note-taking harder, but social acceptance was more challenging. The boys swarmed around Melanie and paid little attention to Alana. As I asked students to form into groups, Melanie was immediately asked to join a group. Alana ended up in the same group, but she was asked with reluctance on the part of the other group members.

But there was one other huge difference between the girls that wasn't as easy to see and took time to reveal itself. That difference was in their attitude.

Each day Melanie came in with a frown, complaining about the homework, complaining about her bad day, and basically complaining about everything. On the other hand, the first thing Alana always did when she came in was tell me what she was thankful for.

"Professor Howard," she would say, "that was a tough homework assignment. I'm grateful you assigned it so I could learn it." One day she said, "Isn't it a beautiful day? The sun is shining and warm, and it just makes me thankful to be alive." The next day it was snowing, and she said, "Don't you like the snow? I am so grateful for the sparkly landscape."

This had been going on for over half the semester. Melanie, with everything going for her, was dismal and complaining. Alana, with her many challenges in life, was smiling and happy. But there was something else I noticed. As the semester wore on, the other students were gravitating away from Melanie and toward Alana. This included the boys. They would rather be with Alana and her sunny attitude than with Melanie and her good looks.

I dreaded Melanie's daily report of gloom, but I always looked forward to Alana's happy thankfulness. One day the weather was frigid, the sidewalks were slippery, and the sky was gray. Melanie came in complaining about it all, as usual.

A little while later, Alana came in, smiling, and said, "I am so grateful that the weather changes and adds variety to life."

I laughed. "Alana, you always come in smiling and tell me what you're grateful for. Is there a reason?"

She smiled and nodded. "My mother always taught me that it's hard to feel sorry for yourself if you find something to be grateful for. And when you're grateful, life is always better. She always says, 'There is nothing so bad it can't be made worse by complaining and nothing so good it can't be made better by gratitude.'"

Melanie was suddenly very quiet, and I could tell that she was thinking about what Alana said. As the days went on, Melanie complained less and less. Then one day, about a month before the end of the semester, Melanie came in and said, "The snow crunched beneath my feet all the way here. I'm grateful for fun, crunchy snow."

Gradually, more and more, Melanie told what she was thankful for. But on the last day of class, I realized how much of an impact Alana had made on Melanie when Melanie said to me, "You know what, Professor Howard? I'm even grateful for math."

34

An Independent Child

Our neighbors have a little three-year-old daughter, Millie, who is very independent. She has to do everything herself, and she has been that way since she could barely crawl. Her first words were probably, "Do it self," because that's what she always said.

One time when we were at church, she was standing in front of the water fountain, which was about a foot above her head.

"Do you want some help to get a drink?" I asked.

"Do it self," she replied.

She thought and thought and considered all options but could not figure out how to get a drink. She finally let me lift her up to the water. But the minute I went to push the bar that made the water come out, she said, "Do it self," and pushed it on her own.

In the church nursery, she was the same way. I opened the toy cupboard, and the toys were stacked on the shelves as they always were.

"Which toy would you like, Millie?" I asked.

She pointed to a bear positioned a couple of feet above her head. I reached for it, and she said, "Do it self."

I rolled my eyes but left the bear where it was and started to hand toys to the other children. Millie stood on her tiptoes, but she was still nearly a foot short of reaching the bear. The other children started playing with their desired toys while Millie stared at the bear, trying to figure a way to get it down.

She took a small doll, laid it down on the floor, and stood on it. She still couldn't reach the bear. The doll underneath her feet rolled, and she fell. I reached down to help her up, and she said, "Do it self."

I sighed and let her stand up on her own. Millie looked around and saw a little stick that the children used to make a corral for the toy

35

farm animals. She got the stick, took it over to the shelf, and tried to reach the bear with it. Waving the stick, she realized it was about an inch short. After thinking for a minute, she went and got the doll again. She stood on it and waved the stick, barely touching the bear, but it was enough to unbalance the bear, sending it toppling to the floor.

I smiled. I had to admit Millie was quite innovative. Some of the other children wanted us to do everything for them, even what they could do for themselves. But Millie's attempts at doing everything for herself taught her to think. I realized this even more as the weeks went by. I watched as Millie became more and more clever in her ability to do everything. A month or two later, I was standing by the water fountain lifting each nursery child up to get a drink.

When Millie came, knowing her temperament, I waited for her to ask. But she didn't ask. Instead, she disappeared into a nearby classroom and came out dragging a child-size chair. She scooted it up next to the water fountain, climbed on it, and got her own drink. She didn't bother returning the chair, so I did, but I marveled at her ingenuity.

Sometime later that day I ran into Millie's mother. I told her what I had observed about Millie over the last few months and what I had observed earlier that morning.

"Have you also noticed that none of her clothes ever match?" Millie's mother asked.

"I haven't," I replied. "But that's probably because I don't notice such things."

Millie's mother sighed. "Well, they never match because Millie insists on dressing herself. I'm considering getting rid of all of her shirts and blouses and replacing them. And you know what they'll say?"

"What?" I asked.

"They will say, 'Mom loves me, but I dress myself.'"

Giving of Self

Christmas was fast approaching, and as I sat in church, all I could think about was the many things I needed to do. The lesson was titled "Caring and Sharing," but I heard little of it. Then the teacher said something that caught my attention. "As you rush through your busy life this time of year, remember what this season is all about. It is about giving. And the most important thing you can give is your time to those who need it."

I pondered that through the rest of the lesson. As we got to the end, the class leader asked if there were any announcements or needs in our community. Dean, an old veteran, was sitting on the bench ahead of me. He slowly struggled to his feet.

"There's a Christmas dinner for those of us still living who served in World War II. I would really like to go, but I can't drive. It's about an hour south of here, and I was wondering if anyone might be going down that way on Tuesday evening."

I thought of my father, also a World War II veteran. He had passed away, and I wished I could take him to that dinner so we could visit again. The room remained quiet for some time, and Dean sadly sat down. As he did, he said, "I didn't think so, but I thought I'd ask."

I thought of my father again, and I patted Dean's shoulder. "I'll take you."

He looked up, and I could see a slight glimmer of tears in his eyes. "Really?"

"Sure," I replied. "I'd take my dad if he were here, so I'll take you instead."

The next day I worked as hard as I could. I also worked hard on Tuesday morning. But it seemed that the harder I worked, the more

I fell behind. But the appointed time arrived, and I left work to pick Dean up. He was anxiously waiting.

He smiled as he climbed into my van. "I was afraid you might have forgotten."

"I didn't forget," I said. "I just had to finish up some things at work."

"It's so nice of you to take me. I haven't been to one of the reunions in a while, and the guys I fought with on Okinawa are starting to pass away."

"You fought in Okinawa?"

He nodded. "It was bloody, and I lost a lot of friends. We paid dearly for every inch."

As we traveled, he told stories about the friendships he'd built during basic training. He shared what it was like to go home for one last visit before shipping out to the Pacific, knowing he may never see his family again.

Next, he talked about crossing the Pacific. "Often the men would joke and act brave, but deep down we were all scared to death. As we approached Okinawa, everyone was quiet. It was impossible to joke or feel anything but scared for what lay ahead."

He was quiet for a brief time, and I waited. When he started to speak again, his voice quivered. "While the fighting was going on, your mind was only on two things: doing your job and staying alive. Everything seemed to happen fast and slow at the same time. But the hardest part came after the fighting was over. I was assigned to help bury the dead. Some of them were men I'd been talking to just days earlier."

Dean talked all the way to the dinner. I was invited to join the veterans as Dean's guest, and he introduced me to some great men. On the way home, Dean told more stories. When I dropped him off, he said, "Thank you for taking time for an old man like me. I'm sure before the year's up, some of those men will be leaving to join our fallen comrades."

Words could not express the honor I felt to take him, though I tried. And I was glad I took time to spend that evening with Dean because only a few weeks later, I was paying honor to him, for it was he who left to join his fallen friends.

Markers

As a scoutmaster, I tried to make sure that we went on at least one campout every month, even in the winter. We used these weekends to teach the boys survival skills. But one particular winter month, the boys begged to have their campout in the cabin Gordy's grandparents owned.

"Staying overnight in a cabin doesn't really constitute camping," I told them.

"But maybe we can just make this a fun time," Gordy replied.

"I'm trying to make men out of you. That's a tough assignment," I teased.

"Ha ha ha," Gordy replied. "Thousands of comedians out of work, and we get stuck with you."

The boys looked at me hopefully. I turned to my assistant, Rod, and he shrugged. "Maybe there are times for just good old fun and camaraderie."

"Okay," I said. "But I expect you all to be on your best behavior. I don't want Gordy's grandparents having any reason to wish they hadn't invited us."

"Hey," Gordy replied. "Don't worry about it. I'll be there."

"That's exactly what I'm worried about," I said.

"Ha ha ha," Gordy replied. "Thousands of comedians out of work, and I'm still stuck with you."

All the arrangements were made, and Gordy got the key from his grandparents. On Friday evening, we all loaded up and drove to the cabin. As we traveled along, Gordy pulled out some markers.

"What are those for?" Devin said, laughing. "Did you bring some coloring books, too?"

"Nah," Gordy replied. "These are to color your face when you fall asleep."

"What about you?" Mort asked. "We could do it back."

"I plan to stay awake all night," Gordy replied.

When we finally arrived at our destination, I was shocked. "Gordy, I thought you said it was a cabin. This is nicer than my home."

"That's because you built your home," Gordy replied.

"Ha ha ha," I replied. "Thousands of comedians out of work, and I'm stuck with you."

We had a meal cooked on a gas stove, not over the fire like we were used to. Soon it was time for bed. The cabin was built for big groups, and the loft contained enough bunk beds for all fourteen of the boys who had come. The main floor bedroom had two beds, just right for my assistant and me. We all retired to our beds, but the boys definitely didn't plan to sleep. However, around two in the morning, they finally quieted down. Some time later, I heard our bedroom door creak open. I watched as a shadow moved across our room. I waited until Gordy was poised over me with a marker in hand, and then I spoke in a deep, growly voice.

"How long do you plan to live?"

Gordy jumped back so fast he fell down and crashed into the wall. He slunk his way to the door. As he was closing it, he whispered for me to hear, "It was just a dream. It was just a dream."

"Go!" I said, and he shut the door.

The next morning, as the boys wandered down bleary-eyed for breakfast, every one of them had red, blue, and green lines on their faces—everyone but Gordy. He had stayed awake all night. But by three o'clock in the afternoon when we headed home, he couldn't keep his eyes open. The other boys slid the markers out of his hands, and he woke just enough to tell them to give them back. But instantly he was back asleep. As they colored him, he would wake only for an instant now and then and quickly fall back asleep. By the time we arrived home, there was not one inch of his face, hands, ears, or any other exposed skin that wasn't colored.

The next day, the boys wandered into church, the permanent marker barely removed. The congregational leader grinned and said, "You boys look colorful today."

Gordy rolled his eyes. "Ha ha ha. Thousands of comedians out of work, and we're stuck with you."

The congregational leader laughed. "And stuck with the permanent marker, too."

The Spirit of Christmas

Playing Santa each Christmas helps remind me what this season is all about. People ask me how much I charge, and my answer is always the same. "I don't." Because of how busy I am in December, I can't do many appearances, but what I do, I like to do for free. I enjoy the wonder and joy on the children's faces, and that is my pay.

Usually, I visit big groups, but now and then, if a child needs a special visit, I try to make time for it. One particular Christmas, a mother called and talked to my wife, Donna. The lady said she had a little son named David who had extreme autism. He was almost five years old and had hardly said a word. He lived in his own world and seldom let anyone else into it. She told my wife that David desperately wanted Santa to come visit. That wish was one of the few things he had ever communicated to anyone.

When I arrived home, Donna told me about her visit. I looked at my schedule and didn't think I could possibly squeeze in one more thing. But as I continued to think about this little boy, I knew I needed to take the time, so I requested more information. The mother gave Donna the names of each of her children, their ages, a brief description of each one, and something particular about what each child wanted. I mainly wanted to know about David—what he liked, what he hoped for from Santa, and whatever other details I could get. David's mother said he especially liked toy cars. He thought it would be the most wonderful experience in the world if Santa would bring him some toy cars and play with him.

Donna wrote the information down, and I spent some time memorizing it. The mother promised she would have toy cars sitting in the living room. She also said she would have presents for each of the children in the mailbox.

When I arrived, I went to the mailbox and collected the gifts. Then I started jingling the bells I was carrying and knocked on the door. When a girl opened it, I thought of the children's descriptions and decided she must be the ten-year-old. I hoped I was right.

"Hello, Mary, how are you?"

She gasped and ran to the other room. I heard her say to her older sister, "Santa's here."

"Santa doesn't exist," the older sister said.

"Well, he knew my name."

"Big deal," the older girl said. "I know your name, and I'm not Santa."

They came to the door with the older girl in the lead, and I said, "Hello, Susan." She rolled her eyes, so I said, "I hope you still want that stage makeup for your part in the school Christmas play." Susan gasped and covered her mouth. Then I mentioned something personal to each of the other children, including the baby sister. I handed out the presents, and the mother, who stood by grinning, told the children they could open them. Susan's had stage makeup, and each child, likewise, unwrapped an item I had dropped a hint about.

Finally, it was David's turn. He opened his present and found toy cars.

"You know what?" I said. "I love toy cars. I see you have a roadway, a garage, and everything. Can I play cars with you?"

David nodded and handed me a couple. I sat on the floor, and we raced them around the roadway and in and out of the garage. Meanwhile, the other children, especially Susan, stared at me.

After a brief time, I finally stood. "Well, I guess I better go visit some other children."

David ran to me and hugged my waist. I patted his head and said, "You be good, and we'll have something more for you in a couple of weeks."

He nodded and hugged me again. I went on my way, feeling like I had once again been the one who was truly rewarded.

A few days later, I saw a posting on Facebook by the mother. She said that after I left, David had called his grandparents. He told them all about his experience. And even though no one understood most of what he said, they did understand when he said, "Santa come play cars me."

And I smiled as I once more remembered that all of us carry a little of the spirit of Christmas when we give of ourselves.

Snowed In

It was only a week before Christmas that year when the big snowstorm came. Once it started, it didn't stop for a long time. A foot of snow dropped that first night. The snow plows quickly cleared it away, disappointing the children who had to go to school. But as the snow kept coming, the snow plows couldn't keep up, and the children were thrilled to get a couple of extra days of Christmas break.

But the excitement wore off as the snow continued and people grew weary of shoveling. Out in the rural area where we live, some people desperately tried to get out for a last little bit of Christmas shopping. But most didn't make it far beyond their driveways before they had to turn back.

Once the snow reached a depth of about three feet, a strong wind kicked up, blowing snow over the roads in drifts that were ten feet high in some places. The county officials announced that all nonemergency road clearing would be discontinued until after the storm ceased. Authorities suggested that no one venture out unless it was an absolute emergency. Soon power went out and phone lines went dead.

Our family was quite comfortable. Though we usually used electric heat at night, we used a wood stove during the day. It became our only source of heat and cooking, so we gathered around it and let the storms howl outside. Snow had to be brought in and melted for drinking, washing, and bathroom use. The only real challenge was going outside and taking care of the animals, who were all snug in their sheds. I took care of all outside work and came in looking like a snowman.

Since we had already finished most of our Christmas shopping, we decided that what we had done would suffice. We had a fun

Christmas. We ate lots of candy, read stories, and enjoyed the family togetherness. It was a few days after Christmas when the winds finally stopped. By then everyone had been snowed in for over a week.

The power came back on intermittently, and we learned from the radio that roads were impassible everywhere. The snow was too deep for the conventional snow plows and would initially have to be cleared by the rotary ones. Unfortunately, the county had a limited number of rotary snow plows, and it would take over a week for all roads to be opened.

Over the next few days, the temperature dropped to well below zero. Our family continued on as we had, having limited contact with the outside world. Then one evening, just before New Year's Day, we heard a snow machine. Soon there was a knock on our door. Everyone rushed to see who would be out in this freezing weather. There stood a neighbor who lived about a mile away.

He held out a twenty-dollar bill. "Can I buy a roll of toilet paper?"

I laughed. "A roll of toilet paper doesn't cost twenty dollars."

He sighed. "I've already been to a couple other neighbors trying to buy some, but it seems like everyone is on their last roll and doesn't want to part with it at any price."

"I grew up out in the middle of nowhere," I said. "And I learned to stock up for emergencies like this, so we have extra." I retrieved a whole package and brought it to him. "Keep your money and just replace the toilet paper when you get a chance."

He thanked me and left.

A few days later, after the roads were cleared, the neighbor came up to me at church. "I've got your package of toilet paper in my car," he said. "I'll get it for you right after church."

"What I gave you got you through all right, then?" I asked.

He nodded. "Yes, and I've learned my lesson. When summer comes, I plan to insulate my whole house with toilet paper. I'm not ever going to run out again."

Brothers

I had just moved into the area and was asked to be a clerk helping with the membership of those in our church congregation. One Sunday, I was in the office visiting with the other two clerks when I mentioned Samuel. Samuel was around seventy years old and had just remarried.

"Samuel remarried?" Lane asked.

I nodded. "Just yesterday."

Lane simply said, "Interesting," then walked out.

Harold, the other clerk, shook his head and said, "That's so sad."

"What is?" I asked.

"You're new here," Harold said, "so you don't know, but Samuel and Lane are brothers. At one time they were the closest friends you could ever find. They helped each other plant their farms in the spring, and then they helped each other harvest in the fall. They shared equipment and just about everything else, too. Then, about twenty years ago, something happened. They haven't spoken a word to each other since that day."

I sat and pondered that for some time. I had worked with Lane as a clerk for over a year. I had also been in Samuel's shop and spent time with him doing woodworking. I really liked both men, and it was hard to fathom this division between them. One day, when Lane and I were the only ones working in the clerks' office, I decided to bring up the subject.

"Lane," I said, "Harold told me you and Samuel are brothers. What happened between you two?"

He sat back in his chair and was quiet for a long time before finally speaking. "You know, no one has ever asked me that before.

Everyone just avoids it, afraid to offend me. But I guess because you're new, you don't know that."

"I'm sorry if I offended you," I said.

He shook his head. "You didn't. But the sad thing is, I don't even remember what it was that caused the problem. There was some little thing, and it just seemed to grow bigger and bigger. It was all so stupid."

I didn't say much more. Instead, the whole time we worked that day, Lane talked all about himself and Samuel as young boys. They had obviously not only been brothers but also best friends.

Some time later, visiting with Samuel, I had a similar experience. These two men couldn't even remember the wedge that separated them, but when I asked them why they didn't become friends again, they both said basically the same thing. They didn't know how.

A short time after that, in the icy cold of January, Samuel went out to feed his cattle and fell, with a hay bale landing on top of him. He injured his back and couldn't move. His wife found him almost frozen to death and rushed him to the hospital. Through the family grapevine, Lane heard about it. Samuel's wife called some men in the community asking if we could take care of the cattle, but when we went over there, the work was already done.

Lane came to greet us and smiled. "Samuel's my brother. I'll take care of everything."

And Lane did take care of everything for months, well after the time Samuel came home. Their friendship renewed, and they became best friends again.

About five years later, Lane passed away. At the funeral I patted Samuel's shoulder and offered my condolences. He said, "It was all so stupid. My biggest regret is the twenty years that we could have been friends but wasted it on something we can't even recall."

Samuel has now gone to join Lane, but the memory of them comes back to me each year as I make my New Year's commitments. I always vow to put away hard feelings so I don't end up with regrets in place of friendships.

Teaching Children about Service

My friend Richard saw me and laughed. "Is this the new you?"
I tried to act innocent. "What do you mean?"

He laughed again. "Your eyebrows are missing, and so is most
of your hair. And you're redder than a lobster."

I sighed as I thought about my new appearance. I always
looked for chances to teach my children about community service, so
when I heard there was a need for volunteers to help maintain the
church furnace, I was quick to sign up.

Our old church had a coal furnace. The coal had to be raked
down over the auger that fed the fire, and all of the old clinkers had to
be cleaned out of the furnace.

A few days before it was my turn to take over the furnace, I met
Gary at the church. He was the current volunteer, and I wanted to go
through the routine to make sure I knew where all of the switches were
and learn any other details. It had been a long time since I'd removed
clinkers from a furnace.

Clinkers are the debris left over from burning coal. They look
like strangely shaped rocks. If a fire has been burning, they will still be
white hot. To clean out the clinkers, I had to reach into the furnace
with a long metal rod which had a handle on one end and two pincers
on the other. When the pincer end was over a clinker, I had to twist the
handle end, closing the pincers and grasping the clinker. Then I'd pull
the hot clinker out of the furnace and drop it into a metal bucket.
When I was a boy, we had a coal-fired furnace, so I had done this many
times.

Gary showed me the switches to shut down the auger and the
blowers, which blow air through the furnace to make the fire hotter and
put more heat into the building. When I first started on the clinkers, it

took a little practice to grasp them properly. But I quickly had the hang of it and soon had the furnace clean. Then I restarted the auger and the blowers.

After I had done this by myself for a few days, I decided it was time to teach my six-year-old son. I hoped he would learn community service by following my example.

He was fascinated as we went down into the old furnace room. Everything was new and exciting to him. I told him our first job was to rake coal to the auger. I turned to grab a rake, and when I turned back, he was nowhere to be seen. When I called his name, he called back to me from the coal bin. We weren't actually supposed to climb into the coal bin. We just reached over the short wall and pulled the coal down. By the time I got him out, both he and I were black from one end to the other with coal dust, and I knew my wife wouldn't be happy.

Next came the clinkers. I shut off the switch to the coal auger and pulled the handle down to shut off the blowers. My son intently watched the whole process. Then I opened the furnace door and reached in to grab a clinker. As I did, I explained what I was doing.

"Once I reach this into the furnace," I said, "I turn the handle to grab a clinker."

When I said "turn the handle," my son thought I was telling him to do something. But the only handle he could see was the one that turned on the blower fans. So, wanting to be helpful, he turned them on. When the air from the fans hit the inside of the furnace, a ball of fire shot toward me. Before I could move, the fire hit the coal dust all over me, taking off my eyebrows and most of my hair.

As my thoughts returned and Richard grinned, waiting for my reply, I managed a weak smile. "It's the look that comes from teaching a child about service."

Quick Wit

I attended the funeral of my uncle Delos this last week. He was a good man who loved and served other people his whole life. His wife, Betty, was his greatest love, and when she died about ten years ago, his life was lonely and empty.

Delos kept himself busy to avoid thinking about the emptiness he felt without Betty. He grew a big garden, including a large raspberry patch. He didn't need most of the food he raised and gave almost all of it away. He spent even more time doing service. If anyone was sick, needed a visit, or could just use a friend, Delos was there.

But then his life took another downward turn. His health started to deteriorate. His mind was still alert, but he physically couldn't do all the things he had been doing. He had to give up growing his big garden, and he couldn't visit others without someone to take him. It was at this point that he went to live with his son, Brent. Delos loved to read and learn, and he still spent time doing that. But he missed doing the work he loved and visiting people. Even worse, he missed Betty more than ever.

One day, another of his sons, David, called. "Dad," David said, "There's an agriculture show up in Idaho. Would you like to go?"

If Delos was anything, he was a farmer. Once people are farmers, their hearts never leave it behind. The thought of seeing the newest tractors, combines, and other types of modern equipment was exciting. He happily accepted the invitation.

On the appointed day, Delos was awake early, even earlier than he used to get up to milk cows. He was dressed and waiting for a couple of hours before David arrived. Once Delos was in the car, they started the three-hour drive to Idaho. There were two things that Delos liked to do as he traveled. He liked to read road signs and comment on them, and he liked to tell stories.

"Oh, look at that. Welcome to Carterville, population 315. By the looks of things, I'm sure they must have also counted the cows to get that number. Hidden Road. Ha ha. We found it, so it's not too hidden. Oh, hey! Look at that. Dave's Burger Barn. I remember when Betty and I were first married. I took her with me to go fishing, and we stopped there to eat. It was a lot newer place back then. Burgers cost fifteen cents. I bet you couldn't find a burger for that price anymore."

As they traveled along, David listened to his father read signs and tell stories. Most of the stories brought back memories of Betty and the times she and Delos had spent together.

When they arrived at the agriculture show, David pulled the wheelchair out of his car and helped his dad into it. David wheeled his father to every exhibit. Delos was like a child in a candy shop looking at all of the new equipment. He wanted his picture taken next to a tractor so everyone could see the size of it compared to his wheelchair. As the day came to a close, Delos, though tired, was reluctant to leave.

As they traveled along back to Brent's house, Delos didn't read signs or tell stories. He was just quietly thinking. After some time traveling in silence, Delos spoke quietly.

"You know, David, I can't wait until I can be with your mother again."

David had a sense of humor that he had inherited from his father. He chuckled slightly and said, "Dad, what if Mom makes it to heaven and you don't?"

Delos might have been old and slightly infirm, but his mind was still sharp. He laughed and said, "That's okay, David. If I don't make it to heaven, I'll just come and live with you."

The Avid Scouter

My uncle Delos was an avid scouter all his life. From the time he turned twelve and joined his first Boy Scout troop, he never missed a campout. Even after he moved into the group of older boys, he still volunteered to go on campouts with the younger scouts. He was only seventeen when he was asked to be the assistant scoutmaster. He happily agreed.

The boys loved and respected Delos, partly because they knew they were important to him. He expected a lot from them. He not only insisted they know their knots but also taught the boys to survive under any circumstance. A few times the boys claimed the skills Delos taught them had saved them.

But then came the Japanese bombing of Pearl Harbor, and soon Delos's number came up for the draft. He was not the only one being called away. Almost all of the men were drafted, leaving the scouts with no one left to be their scoutmaster.

Delos went away to basic training. As he marched, drilled, and did calisthenics, he thought of the boys in his troop. There was no one there teaching them to tie knots, no one taking them camping, no one eating the burned food they made, and no one sitting around the campfire telling them stories. As he approached the end of the first training, the soldiers were told they were going to receive a short leave. It was only for one long weekend, and then they had to be back for more training.

Most of the men planned to visit the nearby town and live it up, but Delos decided on another plan. Late Thursday night, he called home and told his family to have the boys meet him at the train station with their packs and camping gear. Then he left to board the train home. He traveled all through the night, arriving at the train station in his home community early Friday morning.

Delos wasn't sure if everything would work out or if the boys would even be there, but when he stepped off the train, there were the boys with their packs and gear, along with the one thing Delos never went camping without—his guitar. Other community members were also there, ready to drive the troop members to the designated campsite. Off they went into the woods. They had the usual burned food and sat around the campfire telling stories. The boys listened intently as Delos told them about basic training and shared his love of country.

Then Delos pulled out his guitar and sang patriotic songs. He also sang "I Am My Own Grandpa" and other old-time favorites. All too soon, it was Saturday evening, and the community members were back to take them home. The boys all loaded into the cars, tired, dirty, and happy. Delos rode back to the train station, where he enjoyed a visit with his family before boarding the train back to the base.

Delos once more rode through the night to get back. As he walked into the barracks on Sunday evening, most of the men were still nursing hangovers. When Delos sat on the edge of his bunk, one of the other soldiers sniffed the air.

"Is that you that smells like a campfire?" the soldier asked Delos.

Delos smiled and nodded. "I rode the train home and took my scouts camping."

"That's crazy," the other soldier said. "You could have been out drinking and having fun."

"I was having fun," Delos said. "But while I was having fun, I was also making men out of boys. And there's nothing better than that."

A Cat and a Dog

When I was invited to a charter school to speak to the students about writing, I had a fun day sharing stories. It was my first experience speaking to a whole school, two grades at a time. The older students, junior high age and older, didn't want to ask questions. They just wanted me to tell them stories. But the younger children all wanted to tell me a story with me after I shared one with them.

I loved listening to them. The children had read one of my books in their classes, which was about a boy and his dog. When I told some stories from that book, a precocious seven-year-old girl named Tanya waved her hand excitedly.

"We had a dog and a cat that hated each other," she said. "They were both the same size, and they were always fighting. Sometimes one would win and sometimes the other one would. Then one day our dog had twelve puppies. There were so many that she couldn't keep them all full. She didn't have enough milk, and she would barely get some fed when the others were hungry again. Most of the time the puppies were hungry, and we had to help feed them with a little dolly bottle.

"A few days after our dog had her puppies, our cat had kittens. She was out in our garage, and some neighbor dogs snuck in and killed the kittens. That made our cat hate our dog even more. She seemed to blame our dog for the loss of her kittens and was jealous of the puppies.

"One day, our dog was so tired from always feeding the puppies that she fell asleep in her basket in the kitchen. We watched the cat sneak in through the doggy door and take a puppy out to her basket in the garage. She kept coming back for more, taking them out to her basket. We didn't know what would happen if the dog woke up. But the dog didn't wake up until after every puppy was gone.

"When she did wake up and couldn't find her puppies, she was upset and searched everywhere. But once she calmed down, she smelled around and followed the cat's path to the garage. We had gone out to the garage to watch what would happen.

"The cat was ready. She had climbed up on the stair rail and jumped on our dog when she came out the doggy door. They fought like crazy, and we finally had to step in to stop them so they wouldn't kill each other. We started to take the puppies back to the kitchen, but once we had taken half of them, our cat started hissing at us and wouldn't let us near the others.

"That's when my mom had an idea. She said that maybe the cat would nurse the rest of the puppies, and we wouldn't have to help feed them. Dad said that was crazy, but we left half of the puppies with the cat. We did have to lock the doggy door so the cat wouldn't steal the other puppies, and so the dog couldn't get out to get the ones the cat had.

"The cat did nurse the puppies. And after the puppies had their eyes opened, we unlatched the doggy door and let them go back and forth. At first, the cat would hiss at the dog, and the dog would bark at the cat, but eventually, they started getting along, and the puppies would nurse from either mother. It was weird seeing the dog and cat lying next to each other, both nursing the puppies."

"That's a fun story," I said. "Did you get any pictures?"

Tanya shook her head. "My dad always thought it was too weird. But now he says he wishes he had made some videos."

"Why?" I asked.

"Because he says if he had, we could have put them on Youtube and we'd be rich."

Exponential Growth—Or Not

In my math class, we had been studying exponential growth in my math class, including how interest grows and doubles investments. One of the concepts we talked about was doubling.

"If you had a penny the first day, two the second, four the third, and eight the fourth, how much would you have in thirty days?" I asked.

The students worked in their groups. They decided on a pattern for the formula, worked the problem, and eventually had answers. I called on one group, and the girl chosen as the spokesperson answered.

"It would be $5,368,709.12," she said.

"That's correct," I replied. "Now, let's try something more practical. Money doesn't double every day. But what if you invested five hundred dollars each month. What would your growth be if you were also making seven percent per year in interest?"

I showed them the formula for investment with interest growth and let them work in groups again to calculate the answer. They calculated the amount for thirty years and got more than six hundred thousand dollars. Then they did it for forty years and got well over a million. They were excited to think that they could make that much money for retirement.

"The main thing," I said, as class was ending, "is to invest early and consistently."

Many of the students seemed impressed by what they learned. They went on to do their homework, which included thinking of examples of exponential growth.

At the next class, a young man named Seth approached me and told me he had the best example of exponential growth. He asked if he could share it with everyone. I always like it when students come up with good examples, so I told him he could. He walked up to the board, turned, and faced the other students.

"There's a national contest for math and engineering projects," Seth said. "The winner receives a thousand-dollar scholarship. I've entered it, and I think I have one of the best entries. The problem is, I can't win just by having the best project. I have to get the most votes."

Seth then turned to the board and wrote a web address there, along with his name. "I would like to have everyone go to this web address and click on my name. You can read all about my project and vote for me. You will have to put in your email to vote because they use it to make sure each person only votes once."

Seth then motioned to me. "Do you remember that thing about pennies doubling and exponential growth that Professor Howard taught us last time? Let's see if we can get it working on this contest because it would be the perfect example of what he talked about. If all of you would go to your apartments and get your roommates to vote for me, and then if all of them got their roommates to vote for me, and then if all of them got their roommates to vote for me, and so on, my votes would grow exponentially."

The class members were all nodding and agreeing that this was a good example and would be a good idea. Meanwhile, I stood off to the side, trying to keep from smiling. I must not have done a good job of hiding my amusement, because one of the students asked, "Professor Howard, is something funny?"

"I hate to ruin any excitement on an example of exponential growth," I answered. "But your roommates would have the same roommates you do."

As it started to dawn on each of them what I was saying, they began to laugh at themselves. Seth said, "Oh. I guess that wouldn't work as well as I thought, would it?"

"No," I replied. "But it sure sounded good."

Reputation

I was a senior in high school, and it was just two weeks before Valentine's Day when Lisa called me. We were cousins, close in age, and good friends.

"Daris, are you free the Saturday after Valentine's Day?" she asked.

I knew I didn't have a wrestling meet that weekend, and I also knew I didn't need to check my social calendar, because I didn't have a social life.

"Sure," I replied. "What do you have in mind?"

"I have a friend named Tina," she replied. "And she said she'd set me up on a date to the Valentine's formal if I'd set her up with you."

"Do I know her?" I asked.

"No. But I told her I had a good looking-cousin, and she was excited."

"Have I ever met your good-looking cousin?" I asked.

"Very funny," she replied. "But would you be willing to go? We could probably work out for you two to meet ahead of time."

Lisa lived in a bigger town about forty-five minutes away. We talked about ways I could meet Tina, and I suddenly remembered something.

"Hey, Lisa," I said. "We're wrestling your school's team down there this Friday. If she could come, that would give us a chance to meet."

Lisa thought that was a good idea. She planned to come and bring Tina.

The day of the meet came, and our team drove to Lisa's school. After weigh-ins, we gathered in the gym. The coach of the other team walked up to me.

"Howard," he said, "I know you've beaten everyone who's come up against you, but tonight your reputation is going down. You're wrestling the fullback of our football team. He's big, strong, and totally undefeated, and he plans to keep it that way." He then laughed and walked away.

"Howard, does that make you nervous?" my friend Lenny asked.

"Not in the slightest," I replied. "There's more to wrestling than just strength."

But with Lisa and Tina watching, I hoped I would win.

That evening, by the time we got to my match, our team was down by ten points with only three matches to go. When my opponent stepped onto the mat, he turned to face the home crowd, and they rose to their feet, cheered, whistled, and stomped.

He and I shook hands, and within seconds after the whistle blew, I had him down and on his back. By the end of the second round, I was ahead fifteen to nothing. I was determined to get the pin in the third. But as I tried to work him into a pin position, he put out his arm. When I tried to force it, he groaned. Twice I backed off to let him pull in his arm, but each time I went again, he did the same thing. I finally decided he must be more limber than I thought, and I pushed on through. He yelled to the ref to stop the match, and we untangled. His shoulder was hurt, and he had to default.

After that, Tina refused to go to the dance with me, feeling I was too mean. So Lisa brought over a girl named Kim, who was very shy. Lisa whispered for me to ask Kim, and when I did, Kim nodded but turned her eyes from me.

The night of the dance came, and Lisa helped Kim fix herself up. I thought Kim was beautiful. Kim's cousin Sam went with Lisa, and we had a fun dinner together. After we arrived at the dance, Sam and I went to get some punch for our dates. When we got back, I found some boys surrounding Kim, teasing her. She was crying.

"I hear your date is a wimpy South Fremont High School boy," I heard one say. "You must be desperate."

The other boys laughed. That was when I tapped the boy who said it on the shoulder. He turned to look at me, his arm in a sling. The shock on his face at seeing me again was priceless.

"How's the arm?" I asked.

Lisa later told me they never teased Kim again.

The Hidden Honeymoon

My son got married this summer. When my youngest daughter's friend Dixie learned of the wedding, she told my daughter a story about Steven, her brother.

Dixie's family had a tradition of trying to get the bride or groom to divulge where they were going on their honeymoon. This could be as straightforward as asking, or as secretive as asking an indirect question, hoping that one of them might slip. In past generations, if one of them did let it slip, the family members were inclined to follow and play some prank on the newlyweds.

Though the pranks had stopped long ago, the game of trying to find out where the couple planned to honeymoon continued, and it had even turned into a contest. The person who found out would win a prize. That is, if anyone could find out.

Dixie said her family members used every wile they could think of to get the couple to tell them where they were going, but Steven had warned his bride, Cindy, about the tradition, and neither of them slipped up all night. When the wedding and the reception were over, the couple left in their decorated car while everyone else stayed to clean up.

The family finished cleaning late in the evening. It was the end of summer, with school starting in just over a week, so the family planned to leave from the reception for a vacation at a resort.

They drove half the night, arriving at their destination at three o'clock in the morning. They were exhausted and ready for some relaxation. They pulled in, and Dixie's dad went to register. After he climbed back into the car, they drove around to the side of the hotel and parked.

That was when Dixie said, "Isn't that Steven's car?"

Everyone looked where she was pointing, and sure enough, it was Steven's car. The "Just Married" banner was a dead giveaway. The family came up with a new game. Their goal was to stay in the same resort for the week and never have Steven or his wife know they were there. As soon as they had moved their luggage into the hotel, Dixie's father went out and moved the car to a parking lot across the street. And then the game began.

The family held a council and decided what they would have to do. When they ate, swam at the pool, or used any other resort amenities at the resort, they posted someone to keep watch. If they saw Steven or Cindy coming, they quickly scampered out another way. They traded off who was on watch so everyone had a chance to enjoy everything. They kept this up all week and had a lot of fun. They were almost caught a couple times, but as the week ended, everyone was sure they had not been discovered.

When it came time to leave, they checked out early in the morning. Dixie's dad retrieved the car from across the street. Everyone was outside waiting, and they quickly threw all their luggage into the van. They drove around the block and then repacked so they would have more room for the ride home. They all promised not to tell Steven or his wife about their little adventure.

They had only been home a few days when Steven and his wife came over for dinner.

"So, where did you end up going on your honeymoon?" Dixie's dad casually asked.

Steven laughed. "It's our secret, and you're never going to know."

The rest of the family laughed.

Dixie said, "And the funny thing is that Steven still thinks we laughed because he was so elusive."

Major Misfire

I sat down to read my email on the first day of the winter semester. "Professor Howard," one of them read. "My name is Shanae, and I'm in your math class. I won't be there today. I hope you won't drop me from your class. I'm not sure when I will get there. We had a family emergency. I don't have any clothes or anything to wear. I know this isn't making sense, but it's a long story. I will explain when I get there. I'll try to get there as soon as I can."

I have received a lot of strange emails from students over the years, and each time I do, I can hardly wait to hear the explanation. It was almost a full week after the semester started before Shanae arrived. She came to class and asked me what seats were available. I pointed out the only one that was left. She sat down, and we started class.

"Shanae," I said, "I had all of the other students introduce themselves the first day, but you weren't here. Would you mind taking a minute to tell us a little about yourself?"

Shanae nodded and rose to her feet. She told us the basic things. She was a freshman, hoping to major in nursing. She told us the town she was from and a few other interesting facts.

"You're starting class almost a week late," I said. "You wrote that the reason you'd be late coming to school was a long story. Is it something you can share with us?"

She smiled and nodded. "It's an interesting story, and it might sound a little strange. You see, my family lives on a ranch that takes up most of a small valley. Our nearest neighbor lives about a mile away. We have to go about forty miles to the nearest town to buy groceries and stuff like that.

"On the other side of the mountain from where we live is a big ski resort. In the winter, almost everyone gets part time jobs in town to help support the influx of people coming to the ski resort. My dad works on the ranch in the summer, but in the winter he works in town at a sporting goods store. My mother works as a waitress in a restaurant for the breakfast and lunch shifts.

"Every morning we all got up and drove to town, and we kids went to school while Mom and Dad worked. But since I graduated, I got a job this winter working at the restaurant with Mom.

"A couple of days before I was supposed to come here, my dad picked up everyone from work and school. When we got home, we found our home had been blown up. Everything was destroyed—our clothes, furniture—everything."

The class gasped. "What happened?" a boy asked.

"We wondered that ourselves," Shanae said. "But we didn't know. The sheriff and the county investigator came, and at first, they assumed it was a gas explosion from our propane tank. But then the investigator found evidence of a mortar shell. Our house had been bombed. The sheriff figured it had been done on purpose and asked us questions about whether we had any enemies, or if anyone would want to kill us. It was scary. We drove back to town and got a hotel room. We didn't dare let anyone know where we were except the sheriff and the investigator.

"We were nervous about going to work or school the next day, afraid that whoever wanted to kill us would come back. But then the sheriff came to the hotel. He said he had found out it was an accident."

"An accident!" a girl in class said. "How does someone blow up your home with a mortar shell and claim it was an accident?"

"Well," Shanae said, "it appears the ski resort was firing mortars onto the hillside to trigger avalanches to make skiing safer. The idiot firing them happened to aim one too high, and it went over the mountain and came down on our house."

I was glad everyone was okay, but I had to admit that she was the first student I knew of who missed class because her family was in hiding.

Contradictions

I walked into a local community library and saw a sign. It said, "If you are illiterate, call . . ."

I couldn't help wondering, "If you were illiterate, how could you read the sign and know that you were supposed to call?" I pointed that out to the librarian, and she laughed. She said she had never thought about it. She decided she would call the number and mention it to them.

This reminded me of some other contradictions I have seen over the years. Some years ago, I purchased a new, external, portable CD drive for my Windows 98 computer. The CD drive attached to the printer port on the computer. When I received the drive, I opened the package and read the instructions. They said to connect the drive, then load the software into the computer to make the drive work. You guessed it. The software was on a CD, which I couldn't use until the software was loaded on the computer.

Recently, our Internet service quit working. I tried everything on my end to get it to work, but to no avail. Finally, I called the Internet provider and asked if there was a problem on their end. The technician sounded exasperated.

"I am so sick of people calling," he said. "I sent out an email telling everyone that our system was down. I wish people would check their email."

"And how are we supposed to do that when our Internet is down?" I asked.

Suddenly, the technician was very quiet. He sounded sheepish when he finally answered. "I never thought of that."

But the biggest contradiction I have probably seen was years ago when the Internet was new. I worked for a government contractor programming Internet-related technologies. This was some time before the Internet became widely known. Later, I also became the Internet director at the university. Because of my experience, I was contacted by a book company editor and asked if I would review a new type of electronic book they were releasing. They were willing to pay me five hundred dollars, so I agreed.

When I received the material, the book was titled, *How to Use the Internet.* It was an online book built across multiple web pages. The information page simply gave a username and a password and said, "Get on the Internet and go to . . ." It had the URL listed there.

I got on the Internet, went to the website, and logged in. The first chapter was all about how to get on the Internet and how to go to a website.

I didn't read more than the first chapter. The contradiction in it drove me crazy. When I wrote my review, I asked, "If readers don't know how to do the things in the first chapter, how can they get on the Internet to read the book?" In all, I only spent about a half hour on the reading and writing the review. I felt guilty spending that short amount of time for that amount of money, so I told the editors they didn't have to pay me.

A couple weeks later, I received a check from the editor, along with a letter. It said, "Thank you, Mr. Howard, for your review. About a dozen people within our company reviewed that book, and everyone thought it was amazing. I know it sounds crazy, but not a single reviewer considered how contradictory it was that readers would already have to know how to use the Internet to access an online book about how to use the Internet. I know you said I didn't need to send the money, but you saved us from an embarrassing mistake, and that is well worth it."

Five hundred dollars for a half hour of work felt almost like a contradiction, too. But I decided if it was, it was one I could live with.

Solving the Real Problem

Kevin came up to my desk after class. "Professor Howard, may I talk to you?"

"Sure," I answered. "What would you like to talk about?"

"I want to wait until everyone else is gone," he whispered.

I nodded, erasing the board and finishing other cleanup tasks as we waited. My class had just finished a test review where I provide questions that the students are to complete and bring to class. Then they go over them in groups to make sure they understand everything.

Once the other students had vacated the room, I sat on the edge of the desk. "So, Kevin, what can I help you with?"

"I'm sorry to keep you after class," Kevin replied, "but I didn't want to hurt anyone's feelings if they overheard me. I wanted to say that I just can't work with my group."

"Personality conflict?" I asked.

That was usually the reason students gave for wanting to change groups.

Kevin shook his head. "No. It's just that they're so stupid I can't stand it. I know all of the answers, and they don't get the math at all. They're no help to me."

"If you know the material, can't you help them?" I asked.

He shook his head. "I don't work well with stupid people."

I was a little taken aback by all this. I've had students who thought they were too smart to work with others, but I never had anyone be so blunt about it.

"Is there any group you would like to be part of?" I asked.

Kevin shook his head. "Frankly, as I listened to all of the groups around me, I realized that they're all stupid. I would be better off doing it on my own."

I paused at his arrogance, but I have learned that someone who doesn't want to work with others shouldn't be forced to—not for the sake of the person, but for the sake of the other group members. It causes too much disharmony.

"If that's how you feel, you don't have to work with a group on the next review."

He thanked me and left. I shook my head in disbelief. I thought about it a minute, and then noted the names of his group members so I could check their test scores later.

A couple days later, after the test closed, I logged in to check grades. The class average was seventy-four percent. Every one of Kevin's other group members scored even higher, receiving an A or a B. I assumed Kevin must have done really well, but when I looked at his grade, I was surprised. He had scored a sixty-two percent.

I said nothing to him, but when I announced the class average, I saw Kevin ask his group members how they did. When they responded, his expression was priceless.

On the next test, he didn't work with his group. Once again, the class average was in the seventies, and Kevin's group members all received an A or a B. Kevin scored a sixty percent. He asked me how his group members did, but I couldn't legally tell him, so he asked them.

After class, Kevin came up to see me. "Professor Howard, do you know what I scored on my two tests?" I nodded, so he continued. "I thought it had to be a fluke for my group members to get an A or a B when I got a sixty-two. I decided they must have dragged me down. But it happened again without them. What should I do?"

"I suggest you study with your group," I replied. "A smart person knows he can learn something from everyone."

Kevin nodded, and the next time we did a review, Kevin actively participated with his group. His test score ended up being a B. He stayed after class the next day to talk to me.

He just smiled and said six words. "A smart person learns from others."

Kevin had learned something even more important than math.

No One Will Notice

When my wife, Donna, came home, I could tell she was upset. When I asked her what was wrong, she broke down and cried.

"I slid on some ice and banged up our pickup," she said.

It was the first new vehicle we had ever purchased. All our others had been used cars I'd struggled to keep running. Donna was especially upset because she was afraid I'd be mad like the husband was of one of her friends when her friend wrecked their pickup.

I went with Donna to inspect the damage. The fender was bent against the tire, so I found a pry bar and used it to bend the fender back into place.

"There," I said. "Almost as good as new. No one will even notice it."

Donna smiled. "That might be a stretch as bent as it is, but it does look better." Then she hugged me, mostly because she was happy I wasn't upset. "Should we get it fixed?" she asked.

I shook my head. "Like I said, no one will even notice it."

I never have been one for fancy cars. As long as the car gets me where I'm going without breaking down, I'm happy. I was just grateful she was okay, and I truly didn't think anyone would notice the bent fender and the dented bumper, because I didn't.

The next summer, I took my son to a little league baseball game. I cheered along with all the other parents. When it was over, we headed for home. I had just turned onto the long stretch of road leading to where we lived when blue flashing lights came on behind us.

I couldn't think of anything I had done wrong. I was sure I had stopped at the stop sign. I wasn't going over the speed limit. I wondered if I had a light out or something. I pulled over as far onto the shoulder of the country road as I could.

The officer came up to the front of the pickup, and I rolled down my window. But he didn't stop. Instead, he walked all the way around the front, keeping some distance between himself and my pickup. He then came up along the passenger side. He stopped and looked specifically at the dent, then nodded his head to a second officer. "Looks like we got the right one," he said.

The first officer walked around to my side again, once more keeping plenty of distance as he came around the front. He came up to my window. Meanwhile, his partner stood near the back and drew his gun.

"Where did you get the smashed fender and the dent in your bumper?" the first officer asked.

"My wife slid off of the road and hit a fence post last winter," I replied.

"Right," he said sarcastically. "Let me see your driver's license."

I was confused by his attitude, but I handed over my license. He looked at it then said, "You actually got the dents from knocking down mailboxes, didn't you?"

That really surprised me, and I told him I most certainly had not.

"We have a report," he said, "of a pickup in this vicinity running down mailboxes, and the description matches yours exactly. We find your pickup is dented in the exact spot where the report said the pickup was dented. And you expect us to believe your wife slid off the road and hit a post? I think you need to step out of the vehicle."

I did as I was told, and as I stood there, he asked, "And what have you been doing for the last hour?"

"I've been with my son at his baseball game," I replied.

The officer looked in, and for the first time, he noticed my son in his baseball uniform. They must turn up their two-way radio when they exit their cars because I heard someone on it say, "Cancel that last call. The person knocking over mailboxes has been apprehended."

The second officer put his gun away. The first officer handed me back my license and said, "I suggest you get that dent fixed."

As I climbed into my pickup, I decided the dent might be a little more noticeable than I thought.

It Can't Be That Hard

＋

Sandy was a young mother with two preschool boys born eighteen months apart. They were like mini tornados. Each day it was all she could do to keep the boys clean and fed. And each day when her husband, Jason, came home, she made sure the house was in order, even though she was exhausted. All she asked for was a little help in the evening so she could relax, too.

But Jason always said, "How hard can it be to take care of the house and two small boys?" Then he'd tell her he had worked all day and was too tired to help.

Sandy was good friends with Jason's mother, so one day she talked to her about it. Sandy didn't want to say anything bad about her husband, so she just mentioned how tiring it was taking care of the boys.

Jason's mother laughed. "That's because they're just like their father. He ran me ragged." She paused for a moment and knowingly asked, "Does Jason help?"

Sandy shrugged. "Not really."

Jason's mother didn't ask any more, but a couple days later she came to visit. "Sandy," she said, "I've signed us both up for a workshop on natural health. It's also a chance for us to do some women things together. It's in a month. We'll leave on a Thursday night, and come home on a Sunday." She then turned to Jason. "You will need to take care of the boys."

"But, Mother," Jason said. "I have to work on Fridays."

His mother was adamant. "Jason, you know you have some vacation time coming, so take a day off."

"You mean, stay home from work and take care of the boys?" Jason asked.

"How hard can it be to take care of the house and two small boys?" Sandy asked.

"Of course I won't have any problem taking care of the boys," Jason said. "I was just concerned about missing work."

Jason seemed confident. And when his mother picked Sandy up for the retreat, Jason assured Sandy that it would be a "piece of cake" for him to deal with things at home.

"I got this," he said.

Sandy enjoyed the weekend. The conference was fun. Between seminars, hair styling and manicures were provided for the attendees. The women swam in the pool and ate wonderful meals. Sandy smiled when Jason called and told her he missed her. She could sense the undertone of panic in his voice as he talked about how all was well at home.

But all good things must end, and the weekend was soon over. As much as Sandy enjoyed it, she was anxious to get home and see Jason and the boys.

When Jason's mother pulled the car to a stop in front of the house, Sandy could hear her boys playing loudly. The two women walked to the house, and the noise grew louder. As they opened the door and stepped inside, Sandy gasped at the sight, while Jason's mother just grinned. Jason sat slumped in a chair. He was unshaven and appeared exhausted. The house looked like a cyclone had hit it. The boys were in their underclothes, sword fighting with brooms.

As Sandy walked on through the house, she found the kitchen sink full of dirty dishes and a disaster of a meal all over the stove, with spaghetti sauce burned in a pan and splattered on the walls and ceiling.

Jason finally pulled himself out of the chair and hugged his wife. "I love you," he said. "Please don't ever go away again."

A few days later, Jason's mother asked how everything was going. "Great!" Sandy replied. "Jason comes home at night and asks what he can do to help."

Jason's mother smiled. "That's the most important training that comes from a women's retreat."

A Tough Lesson

When we were visiting my oldest daughter in California, we stayed with the children while she and her husband went to a concert. While the parents had a great time getting away, we had a wonderful night with pizza, a movie, and playing games.

All too soon the weekend was over, and it was time to head home. We stopped in Provo to drop off my college-student daughter, and then we visited another daughter and her family. We enjoyed playing with our five-month-old grandson as we visited. He was happy and smiling, much different from our last visit. He must have forgotten the immunizations shots he'd had and decided to forgive the injustice he'd been subjected to.

We left there and headed on our way, enjoying the pleasant feelings from the weekend with family. But that didn't last long. As we reached the southern part of Salt Lake City, warning signals were flashing. "Freeway blocked ahead. All traffic routing off of the freeway."

Soon we found ourselves at almost a standstill. We checked the Internet and found that the projected freeway opening was hours away. Then, to make matters worse, my youngest daughter started feeling sick. We got to an open off-ramp lane leading into a mall parking lot. That lane was clear because no one wanted to get stuck in the parking lot. The line of cars there was backed up from one side to the other. My wife drove the van to take her place in the exit line, and I took my daughter for a walk to get some fresh air.

When we returned about fifteen minutes later, our van had only moved ahead about four car lengths. At that point, my wife suggested that we park the van and eat at a restaurant. We finished eating and were sitting in comfort there, watching the line of barely moving cars, when a lady approached us. I was annoyed at this delay that had ruined our evening, and I was in no mood to visit. In addition, she was dressed in rough denim jeans and an old T-shirt and was quite coarse in her demeanor. But the lady seemed driven to find someone to share the time with.

"You know," she said, "it could be worse."

I felt skeptical. How could it be worse?

"You could be the family of the man who was killed in that car wreck," she said. "We may be late getting home tonight. But their husband and father won't be coming home at all."

I felt shame flood over me. She was right. My family was safe, and we still had each other.

"You know," the lady continued, "I lost my father in a car wreck years ago. He was supposed to go to my recital that night. He didn't make it, and I was upset at him. Then, after we got home, the police came and told us what had happened. Suddenly, I didn't care that he wasn't home on time. I just wanted him to come home. I remember watching for him for weeks, hoping it was all a big mistake and that he would still come. But he didn't. Just like that truck driver's family will be wishing for their husband and father, but he won't be there."

As she continued to talk, there were suddenly many things more important to me than being someplace on time. Three of them were with me in that restaurant, and I had spent time with others all weekend. The lady continued to talk, and we mostly just listened. It was easy to tell that this wreck had brought back some painful memories she needed to share.

As the traffic started to move again, and she prepared to leave, I was sad to see her go. As she left, she said, "I should be on my way so my husband will know that tonight I'm coming home."

As we pulled into our driveway at one in the morning, four hours after we had planned, I was grateful for an angel in rough denim and an old t-shirt who reminded me of what is important in life.

No Connoisseur of Style

✦

I am no connoisseur of style. I'm the first to admit that. I realized as much a year or so ago when a student told me my shirt was "so in" and wanted to know where I bought it. I realized it was a shirt my mother had purchased for me in the 1970s. But the realization of how lacking I am in understanding elements of style hit its high point many years ago.

I have taught at a religious university for almost thirty years. One important part of the commitment students sign is to abide by a dress code, which is a slightly higher standard than most schools have. As faculty members, one of our jobs is to remind the students when they start to move away from that standard.

Thirty years ago, just before school began each semester, the student body officers would help those of us who were style-deficient. Some would dress in appropriate clothing and some in inappropriate to help us understand what the new styles were and what was allowed and what was not. As a new, young faculty member, I always relied heavily on these demonstrations. Otherwise, I wouldn't have had the faintest idea what things like culottes were. (For those of you who are like me and don't know, a culotte is a skirt, split like pants.)

As the years went by, the student body officers decided we didn't need to have a demonstration every semester. They cut the demonstrations down to only the fall of the year, with updates sent to us through our department chairman. But then came the electronic age, and administrators decided that instead of having demonstrations, they would just send out an email we could share with our classes.

I will never forget the first one. I was working in my office, finishing up a few last-minute preparations for my class. My email beeped, and the message subject showed it was from the standards office regarding the dress code. I opened it, and in big letters it said, "Read this to your classes."

I quickly printed it off, stuck it with my other material, and returned to my work. I should have read it, but I didn't. I finished preparations for my class just in time. After class had started, I informed my students about the email I had received and read it to them.

"With summer coming, we at the Honor Office would like to remind students of the proper dress code for footwear. Though sandals that buckle around the back of the foot are allowed, flip-flops are not proper dress and are not allowed."

I paused. I had never heard of a flip-flop before except in reference to politicians changing their positions on issues. Reading it concerning clothing was like reading a foreign language. I scanned the note a couple of times to make sure I had read it correctly. Once I was positive I had, I looked up at the class, who seemed to be waiting expectantly for me to continue.

"What in the world is a flip-flop?" I asked.

A girl on the front row held up her foot. "Professor Howard, this is a flip-flop. I didn't know they were against the dress code. I won't wear them anymore."

I looked at what she was wearing and said, "That's a flip-flop? When I was young, we called those things thongs."

The girls blushed and said, "That's not what a thong is anymore."

I learned some important things from my mistakes that day. I learned that if I don't know what something is, I don't ask. I now know what a thong is, and it would probably be better if I didn't. It would at least have been better if I hadn't asked the class what one was.

I learned to read emails before I take them to class. And I also learned that if I don't know what something is, I ask my female colleagues, who kindly explain it to me.

But the biggest thing I learned was that I am the king of all style-deficient people.

A Plan of Discord

Rick was a quiet boy who much preferred reading to being in the thick of things, somewhat unusual for a high school teen. Even though the other students teased him about his love for books, he was big enough that they didn't usually bother him. But one day, before literature class started and before the teacher came, the most obnoxious boys were talking about how much they hated reading assignments.

Steven looked over and saw Rick quietly reading. "Hey, Rick. You like reading so much, why don't you do the book reports for all of us?"

Rick just ignored the comment. Steven was the biggest, loudest, and most obnoxious of the group and didn't like being ignored. He got up from his desk, walked over, and stood right by Rick. The rest of the group followed.

Steven jerked the book from Rick's hand and threw it to the floor. "Did you hear what I said, Mr. Bookworm?"

The other boys stood behind Steven, exchanging smirks. Steven leaned menacingly over Rick, and the others egged him on.

Rick just nodded. "I heard you. But you know very well that Mr. Hodgkin won't let me do your book reports."

Rick reached for his book, but Tyson, another one of the boys, picked it up. He held it up and read the title out loud. "Mythology." He turned to the other boys. "Look, guys. He's reading a book on mythology."

The boys all laughed.

A third boy poked Rick. "Hey, Zeus, where's your lightning bolt?"

The boys all laughed again.

Rick reached for his book, and Tyson tossed it to another boy. Rick reached for it again, and that boy tossed it to someone else. Every time Rick reached for it, that boy would toss it to someone else. Rick felt his frustration rising.

"Guys, can I have my book back?"

"Why don't you fight us for it?" Steven said.

Rick knew he could probably take any one of the boys singly, but he knew he couldn't take all five of them at the same time. Nor did he have any desire to fight. He sat there, considering what to do, when he remembered a story from mythology. It was called "Apple of Discord."

In the story, the goddess Eris threw an apple into the midst of the gods at a wedding feast. The apple was to be a prize of beauty and fueled such a dispute among Hera, Athena, and Aphrodite that it led to the Trojan War.

"Sure, I'll fight for it," Ricks said. "But as tough as you boys are, I'm sure you don't expect me to fight all of you at once. Why don't you decide which one of you is toughest, and I'll fight him?"

Steven stepped forward and stuck out his chest. "That would be me."

Tyson, who now had the book, threw it onto Rick's desk and shoved Steven aside. "Bull, you are. I could whip you any day of the week and twice on Sunday."

A third boy claimed he was toughest, and then a fourth. The fifth boy was smart enough to stay out of it. Soon the boys were shoving each other and yelling. The shoving turned to smacking, and they hit each other harder and harder. Meanwhile, Rick sat down and started reading his book again. Just when the boys were ready to throw punches, Mr. Hodgkin, the teacher, walked in.

He watched the boys briefly, each claiming to be toughest, then yelled, "What's going on here?"

The boys looked sheepishly at each other, then Steven pointed at Rick. "He started it."

"Rick," Mr. Hodgkin demanded, "what do you have to say for yourself?"

Rick held up his book. "I was just reading my book when they came and took it."

"What were you reading?" Mr. Hodgkin asked.

"'Apple of Discord,'" Rick replied.

A slight smile creased Mr. Hodgkin's lips. "Well, maybe somebody learned something from my class after all."

The Not Funny Practical Joke

My daughter, Elliana, enjoys her junior high choir. She loves to sing, and her music teacher is fun. But as with most classes, there are lots of inside jokes. I'm not sure why giving her teacher high-heeled shoes is so funny, but I know it's some class joke, and the uglier, and higher the heel, the better.

In the weeks leading up to the next choir concert, Elliana looked for the oldest, ugliest, most outdated high-heeled shoes she could find. We checked the local thrift shop and even second-hand stores in other towns, but nothing was just right. The concert was drawing near, and neither Elliana nor her friends had found what they wanted. Just a day before the concert, we made one last trip to the store. She looked through the shoe section, but the right shoes weren't there. There were some fairly stylish high heels. But they were too pretty, and the heel wasn't tall enough for the joke.

Elliana was disappointed. But then we saw something that gave us an idea. A store clerk was taking some shoes off the shelves and putting others on. We asked him if there were any shoes that they threw away.

He nodded. "If the shoes on display are ugly or just don't sell, we throw them out to make room for others."

"Can we look at them?" I asked.

He shrugged. "I don't see why not. I probably couldn't just give them to you because my boss wouldn't like it, but I could charge you the minimum price of a dollar."

He showed us a big, fifty-gallon drum at the end of the shoe aisle, where he put the shoes until he hauled them to the dumpster. Elliana rummaged through the shoes. She was almost to the bottom of the barrel when she let out a delighted squeal. She pulled out a pair of pink, old-fashioned high heels. The heels were about six inches tall, and silver chains dangled across the toes. They were about the ugliest things I had ever seen.

She held them up. "Dad, what do you think?"

"I can't believe anyone would wear them," I said. "But since they're at a second-hand store, someone must have. Beauty must be in the eye of the purchaser."

We showed them to the clerk, and he looked at us like we were crazy. "I don't think I can charge you the minimum price for those. How about a quarter?"

I nodded, and he marked twenty-five cents on a tag and put it on them. We took them to the checkout, and the girl there gave us a strange look.

"They're for a joke," Elliana said.

The girl smiled, we paid our quarter plus tax, and we were soon on our way with the perfect prank gift.

The next day was the concert. When it ended, Elliana and her friends invited the teacher to join them at the front of the stage. They handed him the gift bag with the shoes in it. When he pulled the shoes out and held them up, all the choir members laughed.

As people were leaving, a well-dressed lady came up and confronted Elliana. "And just what is so funny about those shoes?"

Laughing, Elliana said, "It's just an inside joke about getting our teacher the ugliest shoes we can find with the most ridiculously high . . ."

Elliana stopped. The lady wasn't smiling, and Elliana suddenly realized the lady was wearing a pair of shoes exactly like the ones they had given their teacher.

"What I mean," Elliana said, faltering for words, "is they weren't necessarily ugly for a woman, but they wouldn't work for a man."

The woman finally left in a huff, and Elliana breathed a sigh of relief. She may have stuck her foot in her mouth, but at least she hadn't stuck her foot in those heels.

It's Time to Go Home

Eva was a big lady. I don't mean she was fat—she wasn't. She was big and strong from years of hard farm work alongside her brothers, and she inherited a good, sturdy frame. She could outwork and out lift most men, and often did. Very few men challenged her on anything, but she wasn't afraid to challenge them. Because she didn't always like to act prim and proper, there were times when her mother reminded her to be a lady. Yet, at the same time, Eva's mother seemed proud of Eva's strength.

Eva's dad also appreciated her strength and willingness to work, especially when her brothers slipped off to play baseball when there were still chores to be done. The boys loved baseball, and far too often in the summer, as evening rolled around, the boys were hard to find.

But things changed one summer. Eva and her three younger brothers had all worked a long, hard day. It was past milking time, and they were tired and wanted to be done for the evening. But since their dad and older siblings were away, it was up to the four of them to do the milking. There was one cow apiece to milk. Eva was gathering the milking buckets when their mother came out to tell them that dinner was ready, and she wanted them to hurry.

It was about then that Eva noticed that the middle brother was gone. Her mother noticed too, and asked where he was. Everyone just shrugged, but they all knew where he had probably gone.

Their mother turned to the youngest boy and said, "You go to the ball diamond and tell him to get back home!"

As her youngest brother headed to the ball diamond, Eva and the oldest of the three boys started milking. She milked her assigned cow and one more by the time her brother finished his. The other boys

85

still hadn't come back, and it was obvious the youngest boy had decided to stay and play ball, too.

Their mother came out to the barn, obviously upset. She told the oldest brother, "You go tell your brothers to get home, or they'll wish they had!"

He headed off to the ball diamond, and Eva started milking the last cow. By the time she finished, none of the boys had come home yet, and she knew the oldest brother must have stayed to play ball, too. She had milked two extra cows, and she was fuming as she finished the chores by herself. When she carried the milk into the house, her mother was there to meet her.

"Eva," she said, "you go to the ball diamond, and you get your brothers. I don't care how you do it. Just bring them home!"

Eva smiled. "Gladly!"

She marched down to the ball diamond, her ire about the extra chores making her more determined. When she arrived at the ball field, it was just as she expected—her three brothers were playing. Their team was out in the field. Eva looked for the oldest of the three, and when she saw him in center field, she started out on the field toward him.

He didn't see her right away because she was coming from behind him, but when he did, he took off running toward home. But he couldn't outrun Eva, and she wasn't about to let him off that easily. She caught him about halfway across the field. She grabbed him, picked him up, and threw him, struggling and kicking, over her shoulder.

She then turned to the other two brothers. "If you two aren't home by the time I get there, I'm coming back for you."

All the other boys on the two teams stared wide-eyed and grinning as Eva passed them. Her youngest two brothers passed her at a dead run and were waiting at home when she arrived. She dropped the oldest boy onto his feet in front of their mother.

And none of the three boys ever again had to be told more than once to get home.

Jobs and Softball

In exasperation, Dean's mother asked, "When will softball ever help you get a job and earn a living?"

Underhand fastpitch softball was big in communities before World War II, and Dean had a crazy fast pitch, with an emphasis on crazy. His pitches were incredibly fast, but they were also all over the place. He and some of his brothers played every chance they got, even when they should have been home working.

Dean's mother had grown weary of it all. More than once, she'd had to dispatch one of her daughters to fetch Dean and his brothers from the ball diamond long after they were supposed to be home. She had learned it did no good to send another brother because he would just end up playing, too.

When the war came, Dean and his brothers were drafted into the army. Dean soon found himself in Europe. When there were breaks in fighting and other army duties, the men organized softball teams. Dean had lots of chances to play. He enhanced his control, and his skill became well known.

Once he came home from the war, there wasn't a lot of time to play ball. It was time to find work and get on with life. He still played when he could, but farm work wasn't high paying, and that meant lots of extra hours.

Some big construction jobs started, and the jobs paid well, but competition was fierce. One big construction firm was building a large commercial lodge at Jackson Lake. They decided to form a fast-pitch softball team among their workers to promote the company and the lodge. But in their first game, they were trounced soundly by a local team.

Those construction managers thought it looked bad for their team to be beaten, especially as badly as they were. They started searching around for better players, and Dean's name came up. A company representative traveled over one hundred miles from the construction site to St. Anthony, Idaho. When Dean was offered a construction job with a much higher wage than his current pay, he jumped at the chance.

In the next game, Dean pitched for the construction crew team, striking out many of their opponents. But there were still holes in his team. Dean watched too many misses by the shortstop when a batter did hit. Dean met with the construction foreman in his office.

"We needed a good shortstop if we're going to have a really good team."

"Do you know one?" the foreman asked.

"My brother, Glen."

"Has he worked construction before?" the foreman asked.

"Not any more than I have," Dean answered.

The foreman turned to his administrative assistant. "Hire his brother."

Glen was hired, and the team did even better. But the catcher couldn't hold on to some of Dean's pitches.

The foreman pulled Glen aside. "Can you catch your brother's pitches?"

"I can if I'm the one who tells him what to throw," Glen answered.

"You work that out with him, then," the foreman said.

The team started doing even better, but they came close to losing a couple times. They were coming up against tougher teams, one of them sponsored by a competitor company. The foreman watched the team and realized that some of his players were good at construction, but they were only mediocre at softball. This time he went to Dean.

"Do you know any other good softball players?" he asked.

"I have other brothers and some cousins," Dean replied.

And that's how Dean's mother came to admit that softball might have a place helping someone get a job after all.

Computer Repair

My phone rang, and when I answered, it was Andy. "Hey, Daris," he said, "can you come help me? My printer isn't working."

It was during the early days of the Internet, and most people didn't know anything about it yet. A teaching salary didn't pay all the bills for my family, so I worked evenings for a government contractor developing technologies that would help lead this revolution. The university where I worked decided to use my skills and have me set up and manage a web server for them. Though I still taught part-time, the university felt the Internet couldn't take much time and made me computer tech for three buildings. I never had a free minute.

During those days, I met almost every person on campus. But about half of my tech-help time was spent in Andy's office. Everyone has heard of the proverbial computer user who thought that his compact disk drive was a coffee cup holder. You might think that no one could be so naïve, but Andy was. In fact, it was only about an hour before Andy's latest phone call when I found this out. It started with his first phone call of the day.

"Will you come over and help me load some new software?" Andy had asked. "It came on some new kind of shiny disk, and I can't figure out where it goes."

"Shiny disk?" I asked.

"Yeah," he replied. "It looks like a vinyl record, but it's smaller and smooth."

"It's probably a CD You just stick it in your CD drive."

I could sense his frustration as he said, "I guess I don't have one on my computer."

I knew he did because I had installed it the previous week. I had very carefully explained what it was, too. I knew it would take longer to try telling him what to do than it would to walk over there. Besides, odds were he'd put it in wrong. Once or twice each week, I had to remove some three-and-a-half-inch floppy disk that he had put into the drive upside down.

To my surprise, when I stepped into his office, the CD drive was open with a mug of pop in it. It was bent down so far it was almost ready to break.

I pulled out the pop. "Andy, this is not a pop holder. It's a CD drive."

"But I have a picture from PC Magazine that shows a coffee cup in it," he said.

He handed me the picture, and I sighed. "Andy, this picture is a cartoon. It's supposed to be a joke."

I handed him the pop and asked him for the CD. He handed it to me, and I showed him how it fit in the drive. I loaded the software and went back to my work. I hadn't been back in my office for more than twenty minutes when I received the call about the printer.

"Did you check to make sure it was on?" I asked.

"Of course," Andy replied. "I'm not stupid."

I thought about all the times I had found that his trouble was just that—he had forgotten to turn on some switch. But I didn't say anything. Instead, I made my way back to his office.

When I got there, I checked, and the printer was on. The light on the printer was green, and the printer had paper in it. Everything seemed okay, but then I remembered that this was Andy. I climbed underneath the desk and found that the printer cable was disconnected from the computer.

"Andy, did you disconnect the printer cable?" I asked.

Andy shrugged. "It was in my way, and I couldn't figure out what it was for."

I sighed, connected the cable, and then climbed out from under the desk. As I was preparing to leave, I saw the pop cup back in the CD drive. I pulled it out and set it on his desk.

I turned to him and said, "And the CD drive is still not a cup holder."

No Good Deed

Maria looked out the back of the truck as they traveled along
through the darkness. She looked at the German soldier resolutely
holding his gun in the ready position. As she considered what lay
ahead, her mind turned back to many years previous at her grade-
school playground. She was only six and had been playing with some
girls when she noticed another girl their age. The girl's blond hair fell
loose over her worn blouse.

Maria pointed to the girl. "I'm going to ask her to play with
us."

The other girls laughed. "Are you crazy? No one wants her."

"That's right," Maria said. "And she needs friends, too."

Maria was the most popular girl in first grade, and the other
girls didn't argue. Maria learned the girl's name was Helga, and Maria
soon had her playing with them. But at lunchtime, Maria saw Helga go
off by herself. Maria watched her and realized she had nothing to eat.

Maria walked over to Helga. "I have extra lunch. Would you
like to share?"

Helga barely raised her eyes but gratefully nodded.

From then on, Maria shared her lunch with Helga every day,
and Helga became one of Maria's best friends. Maria told her father
about Helga, and her father, a good man, searched to learn more. One
night, to Maria's surprise, her father came into the kitchen followed by
Helga's family. Besides Helga, there was her mother, her father, and
two older brothers.

As they ate, Maria's father and Helga's father discussed
business. Apparently, Helga's father's manufacturing company had
been destroyed in the Great War. Maria's father offered to use their
meager savings to finance rebuilding it. As the two girls' fathers stood

and shook hands, Helga's father said, "No good deed ever goes unrewarded."

It was a phrase Maria heard him often say, as over the years the two families became close friends. Helga's father rebuilt his company, and Maria's father prospered from the investment. But then the Nazis rose to power.

"Maria, it's not safe for Jewish families like ours," her father said one day. "We're sending you to college in France."

Away at school, Maria was homesick. But when she found out that Jews were being rounded up in Germany, she feared for her family. Her last letter from her father told her to cease communication and to protect herself. She hadn't heard from her family since. She didn't know if they were safe or not. Then the war came to France, and the Germans started rounding up Jews there.

Maria had heard that Helga's father was using Jews in his factory. Maria wondered how he could do that after all her father had done for them. She also heard that Helga's brothers had joined the German army.

Maria's thoughts came back to the present, and she looked at the German soldier. The image of Helga's brothers came to her, and she clenched her fists. She and the other Jewish girls from her college had been taken in the middle of the night. They had ridden for a day in a train's cattle car and then loaded into this truck. When they stopped at a checkpoint, she heard the driver tell a guard that the truck had "Jewish workers."

Maria had heard the Jews were better off dead than doing slave work. The thought made her hate Helga's family even more. Suddenly, the truck stopped, and she wondered where they were. The soldier ordered them out of the truck. It was the middle of the night with no moon. The darkness was thick around them. In the darkness, a lantern flashed in front of her face, blinding her. Then a voice she recognized yelled, "It's her! We finally found her!"

It was Helga. Maria quickly found herself enveloped in Helga's arms.

As Maria choked out tearful questions, Helga laughed. "Father uses the company as an excuse to take on Jewish workers. Then he sends them to England. A boat is waiting for you and your friends." She handed Maria a paper. "Here's the address where you'll find your family."

As the German soldier escorted Maria to the waiting boat, she realized he actually was Helga's brother.

All bitterness gone, Maria hugged Helga's father before climbing into the boat. As the boat pulled away, he waved and said, "No good deed goes unrewarded."

Too Many Rolls

✦

My wife, Donna, planned to attend a women's conference while I watched the children. We'd been busy with springtime, trying to get the garden planted, so she hadn't had a chance to make bread before leaving.

"That's okay," I said. "If there's one thing I'm an expert at, it's making bread."

That's actually true. In the years before we married, I was an excellent cook. My mother had taught me how to make quite a few things before I headed off to college.

Donna headed off to her women's conference, and I set about running the house. I finally finished feeding the children breakfast, so it was time to make bread. As much as I like bread, I like rolls more, so I decided to make some rolls instead. The roll recipe made between one and two dozen. I thought I ought to double it. I pulled out all of the ingredients, warmed the milk and water, and was just about to add a cup of sugar when my daughter came in and wanted some help fixing her dolly, whose arm had fallen off.

I fixed the doll's arm and then went back to cooking. I wondered which ingredient I was on, the sugar or the salt. I had just remembered I was on the sugar when another daughter came in and showed me a picture she had drawn. I'm not sure what it was, but it was colorful, and I complimented her on it.

She left, and I went back to cooking. I was doubling the amounts in my mind, and I hurried to add the next ingredient before I was interrupted again. I doubled the half cup and put in one full cup of salt. I had no sooner done that when I realized it was supposed to be a cup of sugar and two teaspoons of salt. I looked at the ingredients I had already combined, debating whether to throw it all away and start over or just increase everything. Determined not to waste a cup and a half of milk, I found a conversion chart. One cup is equivalent to forty-eight teaspoons. I would need to increase everything to forty-eight times normal.

I needed to add sixty-nine more cups of milk. At sixteen cups per gallon, that would be more than four gallons. I checked our fridge, and we barely had enough. I found our largest pan and warmed the milk. I found a super-size mixing bowl reserved for family reunions and started mixing. When I began adding flour, the bowl almost overflowed, so I had to separate the dough into other bowls. I finally had it all mixed, and I started rolling out the dough. By noon I had cooked quite a few batches, but I still had pans full of dough. By evening I had cooked most of the rolls.

Around dinner time Donna called to see if I needed anything before she left town.

"Yes," I replied. "We need milk."

"I thought we had plenty," she replied.

"I had to use some to make rolls," I said.

She seemed doubtful but said she would stop at the store and get some. When she finally got home and walked into the house, she gasped. Just about every inch of counter space was covered with piles of rolls.

She looked around and asked, "What happened?"

I explained about the salt, and she laughed. "You were afraid to waste a cup and a half of milk and a little salt?"

She wanted to know how many rolls I had made, so we started counting. We gave up after counting sixty dozen. After we had packed almost fifty dozen into our chest freezer, Donna sighed.

"Next time," she said, "just forget about the cup and a half of milk and start over."

A Band Nerd

Tyson knew what the other band students said about him. They called him a nerd. He did love computers, math, and science. But he also loved band. On the other hand, the students in his computer, math, and science classes called him "Mr. Trumpet." He knew he didn't fit in with either group.

By the first of November, band season was almost over. Tyson was reading on the bus when he first heard about the party a group of the most popular band girls were putting together. He watched as one girl started passing out invitations at the front of the bus, and one girl started at the back. As the girls approached the middle of the bus where Tyson sat, they handed out the invitations more and more discreetly.

Soon they were at his seat and had given an invitation to everyone else. He waited and hoped, but the invitation didn't come. Instead, the girls returned to their seats at the back of the bus. He kept pretending to read, but he couldn't miss the girls' conversation.

"Did you give an invitation to Tyson?" a girl named Shanae asked.

Tyson thought Shanae was the nicest of the girls. She didn't run away from him as much as the others did and would sometimes even say hi. But he knew she couldn't be too friendly without the others making fun of her.

One of the girls laughed at Shanae's question. "Are you kidding? He wouldn't know how to have fun if a computer wasn't involved."

Tyson tried to read, tried to pretend it didn't matter. But it did.

On the next bus trip, something else happened that surprised him. Shanae was crying. He again pretended to read as he listened.

"It's true," Shanae said through her tears. "Those balls on the bus ceiling are cameras."

"You mean that every time we changed on the back of the bus, the cameras filmed us?" another girl asked.

Shanae nodded. "I talked to school security, and they said the cameras recorded us. But they wouldn't delete the recordings. Something about needing them in case anyone asks about improper events on the bus."

Tyson hadn't realized the girls had been changing when they'd sent the boys to the front. He had assumed they wanted to talk about girl things. He thought about the party and told himself the girls deserved it. But he realized that he was still part of the band, and it was his band. He felt some anger at the security personnel for not deleting the videos.

For the next couple of days, Tyson worked every second he could on the problem. He even spent his lunch hours on it. He knew no one would miss him. Eventually, he found what he needed and completed what he set out to do.

The morning of the last band performance, he walked into the band room and handed Shanae a note. He walked away, staying close enough to hear the girls' reaction as Shanae read the note aloud. It said, "The videos from the bus surveillance are erased."

One girl gasped. "Do you think it's possible?"

The girls then headed off to find out.

After they boarded the bus that afternoon, Tyson again listened as they talked.

"When I asked the security officer if the videos were erased, he just laughed," one girl said. "But he tried to look them up, and they were gone. He accused me of hacking them, but he had no proof."

"I don't know who's more surprised—the security officer or us," one girl said. The others laughed.

"I hope the security guards don't find out who hacked the recordings."

From the corner of his eye, Tyson could see the girls all turn and look at him.

After a pause, Shanae stood. "Tyson's a lot better friend to us than we are to him," she said.

She walked to where he was sitting. The other girls followed, and they all smiled at him. "Thanks, Tyson," Shanae said, and the others voiced their agreement.

He just smiled and shyly said, "You're welcome."

And he never missed receiving an invitation to a band party again.

Smiles

We decided to visit the eastern United States so my family could meet some of the wonderful people I knew from when I lived there. From our home in the West, it was a long drive, and there were a lot of new experiences for our children.

As we were driving across Nebraska, my children stared at mile after mile of corn. My six-year-old daughter loved fresh corn out of the garden. It looked like a dream to her.

"Daddy," she said, "can we come here when the corn is ready to eat?"

One night we set up our camp trailer, and I cooked Dutch oven potatoes, hamburgers, and scones. As the sun faded down behind the horizon, the fireflies came out. My children had never seen fireflies before. I grew up in the West, and I had thought fireflies were a myth until I lived in the east. As the fireflies started blinking, our four-year-old daughter, Elli, was amazed.

"Daddy," she said, "there are lots of little blinking stars on our tent. I think they fell out of the sky. Should we put them back?"

I captured one and put it in a jar so my children could see it. It sat quietly, not blinking.

"Can we take it home with us so it can be our star?" Elli asked.

I shook my head. "I'm afraid it wouldn't be happy there. Its family is here."

She agreed that the firefly should stay with its family, so after everyone had seen it, I let Elli open the jar, and we watched it fly away. We sat outside late that night watching the fireflies blink.

One day at our campsite we heard something the children had never heard before. My wife had spent years in Missouri, and she knew the sound well. The noise started out quietly, but as the days wore on, it became an orchestra of sound, like all of nature was coming to life.

"They're cicadas," my wife said.

This time it was my six-year-old daughter, Heather, who was most intrigued.

"What are they doing?" Heather asked.

"They're singing," I replied.

"It's a loud song," she said.

I captured one, an almost impossible task. It sat quietly in the jar.

"How come it's not singing?" Heather asked.

"It's sad," I told her. "It wants to be with its family."

We made sure that everyone had a chance to see the cicada, and then Heather let it go.

Another item of interest was the lush vegetation. Where we live in the West, it hardly ever rains in the summer. We probably get rain no more than once per month. But while we were camping in the East, it rained almost every day. While we were visiting a friend, he said, "I'm sorry it's so dry here for your visit. I doubt it has rained more than three times per week."

My older children laughed, thinking he was kidding, but I told them he wasn't. "You will notice," I said, "that no one has sprinklers."

They sat there and stared for a minute, looking all around at the yards near us. They saw that I was right. They had never realized there were places that didn't need sprinklers.

When our vacation ended, our youngest two daughters could hardly wait to tell their grandmother about all they had seen. It was interesting to hear them explain it in their childhood ways.

"Guess what we saw," Heather told her. "We heard cricketas that were much louder than our crickets here."

"And we saw more corn than even Heather could eat," Elli added.

"And we saw places where no one even has a sprinkler," Heather said.

"But best of all," Elli said, "we saw firestars. And they give light when they smile. But they only smile when they are with their families because families make them happy, just like us."

I couldn't have said it better myself.

Dog Costumes and French Horns

The community musical for the summer was *Chitty Chitty Bang Bang.* I had been chosen to play Lord Scrumptious, the candy maker. It wasn't the part I tried out for, but there was one thing I really enjoyed about it, and that was the children.

After the "Toot Sweet" dance, the children all came in dressed as dogs. They were so cute in their costumes. Since I was the main focus of the scene, even though the dogs were supposed to chase everyone, they all especially liked to bark at me. I always ended up with such a large group of dog-costumed children barking at me that I couldn't run away like everyone else. I feared I would accidentally trip over one of them.

Eventually, the curtains closed, but before it did, many of the smallest children would stand up and run to me. I'm pretty sure they were seeking praise, and I always patted the floppy ears on top of their heads and whispered that they did a good job. During practice, the director then called out, "All dogs must stay on all four paws until the curtain closes!"

But they didn't listen. The whole barking lot of the littlest ones would jump up and race to see who could get to me first. The director tried to compensate by closing the curtains faster. This posed its own problem. In the next scene, the costumed children were supposed to chase the spies across in front of the curtain. But many of them didn't want to proceed with that assignment until they had had their heads patted and were complimented on the good job they did.

I tried to pat the heads of my little canine crowd as quickly as I could, before hurrying them into position for their next scene. Inevitably, there were a few who were late joining the pack to bark their way across the stage.

One particular night, a little five-year-old boy named Gus was quite a bit behind the others. They were almost halfway across the stage when he came out the side door and started woofing his way across in front of the curtain. He was hurrying as fast as he could to catch up, and the orchestra and the audience watched in horror as his floppy hound-dog-eared hat fell down over his eyes.

Gus didn't want to lose any time by stopping to fix it, so he kept going, barking loudly. But his course diverged from a straight line, and he curved toward the orchestra pit. The orchestra members dropped their instruments and grabbed him. The audience gasped as Gus tumbled over the edge. The orchestra members were able to break Gus's fall, and he wasn't hurt. Unfortunately, the same could not be said for the French horn that was dropped and then crushed in the more important rush to save Gus. The violinist pulled Gus's hat back so it didn't cover his eyes, and they hoisted him back onto the stage where he bayed his way on across the stage to the audience's applause.

After those scenes, Gus and I were the only two in the dressing room. He was sitting dejectedly on the bench.

"What's wrong, Gus?" I asked. "Are you hurt?"

He shook his head. "No. But the director is really mad at me. She was waiting for me when I came off the stage."

"What did she say?"

He hung his head. "She said I can't wear my hat anymore."

"She just doesn't want you to get hurt," I said.

"But the hat is the best part of the costume," he replied.

I patted the hound dog ears on top of his head. "The best part of the costume is you, Gus. You are a horn-smashing good hound dog."

He smiled. "I guess I am. The director said something about me being horn smashing, too."

Always Kindness

High school class reunions are always interesting, but my ten-year class reunion was especially so. The women that were trim and beautiful were much heavier. Those of us men who were star athletes, running the mile in around four-and-a-half minutes, now couldn't walk thirty yards without stopping to rest.

Though everyone looked different, we were still able to figure out who each person was. At least, we were until a man walked in, dressed in a Marine uniform with a captain insignia. He was about six and a half feet tall and rippled with muscle.

Lenny, who was also in the Marines, was astounded. "How did anyone become a captain in only ten years?" he asked.

"The bigger question," Rand said, "is who is he?"

No one in our group had any idea. The tall Marine made his way over to the refreshment table and loaded a plate. He visited with people here and there, but even after these brief conversations, no one was any closer to knowing whom he was.

"Maybe he's just a stranger who saw we had food and came to join us," Lenny said.

"Why don't you go tell him that's improper?" Rand asked.

"Are you crazy?" Lenny replied. "I'm only a sergeant, and I thought I was doing well to get to that rank. Besides, he could probably take any ten of us here and put us in the trash can like we used to do to the younger kids."

"My concern," Dallen said, "is whether I ever mistreated him in high school."

Lenny turned to me. "Howard, you never had any enemies in high school. Why don't you go find out who he is?"

That statement was basically true. In first grade, I had been bullied, so as I got older, bigger, and stronger, I tried being kind to those whom others often picked on. I couldn't think of anyone I didn't feel was my friend. So, with the encouragement of the others, I approached the big Marine.

I struck up a casual conversation with him, hoping to learn who he was. I asked him about his family and life. He told me lots of things, but nothing that helped me determine who he was. I could see the last name "Heston" sewn on his uniform. But the only person I knew with that last name had been a small boy named Jesse, who was under five feet tall when we graduated. He was the school wimp. I had stood up for him many times. More than any other boy, he had reminded me of the bullying I received in my painful elementary school years. I looked at this big Marine and knew he couldn't be Jesse.

Still searching for answers, I asked, "How did you rise to the rank of captain so quickly?"

He smiled. "Do you remember the time we were juniors, and I got sick from running the mile in gym class? The seniors were going to make me run another mile, but you told them no. Your confidence and determination made them back down and leave me alone. I've tried to model that confidence and determination and mix it with the kindness you showed me. Kindness and determination have helped me advance. A person can never go wrong with kindness."

I gasped. He was Jesse, and he was at least two feet taller. I took him with me back to the group.

"Hey, guys. You all remember Jesse Heston, don't you?"

I could see by the fear in their eyes that they did. Too many of them had picked on him. Some of the worst offenders cringed and spoke timidly.

Jesse just smiled and said, "It's sure good to see all of you again."

I was grateful that I had tried to be kind to him, even though I could have done even better. We had a nice visit. And after the class reunion was over, there was one thing that always stayed with me, and that was what Jesse had said and had shown.

"A person can never go wrong with kindness."

Appreciation for What We Have

✦

We were talking about Independence Day in my classes when the conversation took an unexpected turn. Most of the class was chattering about fireworks, parades, cookouts, and a day off from class. But Tony sat quietly, saying nothing.

"Tony, are you doing anything exciting for the Fourth of July?" I asked.

"I find Americans strange," Tony replied. "You celebrate freedom without fully appreciating it. There are those like me who are not allowed to immigrate here who would give our lives for what you have. Back in my country, many of my people are dying because we don't have your freedoms."

"What was it like in your country?" I asked.

Tony spoke quietly. "My sister and her husband started a small business. A drug cartel told them that they had to pay some money or they would be killed. They paid what they had, but the drug cartel didn't feel it was enough. So they killed my sister and her husband. Then they went to their home and killed their children. The police did nothing. Many of them were paid off by the drug cartel.

"The drug cartel told my brother and me that they would kill us if we didn't join them. My brother joined, but I loved my sister and her family, and I decided I would rather die than join those who had killed them. So I fled to some relatives, who helped me get a student visa to come here to school."

The class had grown silent as they listened to Tony. His voice quivered as he continued.

"I would give anything to stay and enjoy the freedoms I have experienced here. But I am not allowed to stay. If I go back, I will most likely be killed, and my own brother will probably be given the

108

assignment to do it. This country was built by people like me seeking a place to be free, people willing to die for that opportunity. But now those of us who understand what it means to lose freedom can't stay, while many who have freedom don't appreciate it."

I thought about what Tony had said, and it reminded me of something I had read. I shared it with the whole class.

"Tony said some things that relate to what Chief Justice Roberts spoke about at a junior high graduation this week. He told the graduates that he hoped that at times they would be treated unfairly so they could appreciate justice. He hoped they would sometimes have bad luck so they could be conscious of the role of chance in life and realize success is not completely deserved, and neither is failure. He said he hoped they would experience betrayal so they could understand the importance of loyalty. He also hoped they would sometimes know loneliness so they would appreciate good friends.

"Chief Justice Roberts also said that pain will help a person learn compassion. He told the graduates they were privileged, but they should not act like it. He told them to always say hello to those raking leaves, shoveling snow, or taking out the trash.

"Tony is right. We too often do take the freedoms we enjoy for granted. And Chief Justice Roberts is right that we tend to only appreciate something when we experience its opposite. I hope that doesn't become the case for the rights and privileges we enjoy in this country.

"I hope we don't have to experience hunger and deprivation to appreciate food and prosperity. I hope we never have to see those we love killed in order to appreciate lawfulness. I hope we don't have to experience misfortune to appreciate our opportunities.

"But I especially that we will not have to experience tyranny in order to appreciate democracy. And I pray that we will not have to know oppression to appreciate the freedoms we enjoy."

When I finished, and we started class, I knew that what Tony had shared was of greater value than anything I would be teaching that day.

Sleep

My mother is now ninety-one years old, and her life of long work days is still ingrained in her. I grew up on a dairy farm, and at its peak, we were milking one hundred and twenty cows. The school tardy bell rang at eight-thirty in the morning, so we had to be up by around five o'clock to get the cows milked and fed in time.

My mother was up before we were to make breakfast, and now that she's retired, she's still often on the same schedule. A few times she's decided she needed to talk to me early on a Saturday morning. I am often up before six in the morning, but on Saturday I like to sleep until six-thirty. But now and then, Mom has called me at four o'clock.

One such Saturday morning I answered the phone groggily, my voice cracking.

"Oh, did I wake you?" my mother asked.

"Yes," I said. "We do like to sleep in a little bit on Saturday mornings."

"Okay," she replied. "I will call you back later."

Waking up in the middle of the night makes it hard to go back to sleep. It was almost a full hour before I began slipping into slumber, and just as I did, now only a little after five o'clock, the phone rang again. I answered it and heard my mother's voice on the other end of the line.

"So I called back to talk about what I called about before," she said.

I stretched and rolled out of bed to visit with her in another room so my wife could sleep. I didn't think there was any reason for me to try sleeping again.

More recently, Mom told me about an interesting sleep experience of her own.

"Do you know I go to bed at seven every evening?" she asked.

The last time I went to bed at seven in the evening was a couple of years ago when I was so sick I had the mortician's number on my phone's speed dial just in case. I actually didn't know Mom went to bed that early, but I knew better than to call her much past five.

"I didn't know you went to bed quite that early," I said.

"Well, I do," she continued. "Saturday evening I went to bed as usual, and I immediately fell asleep. When I awoke, I felt more refreshed than usual. I looked at the clock, and it read eight o'clock. I have church at nine, so I almost panicked. I have never slept that late. I hurried and showered and ate breakfast even though I wasn't really hungry. But that isn't unusual at my age. I hurried to church, and you know what I found?"

"What?" I asked.

"I found the whole place empty. There wasn't a car in the parking lot, and every door was locked."

"Did you wonder if everyone had been taken to heaven and forgot to tell you about it?" I asked.

Mom didn't even answer my frail attempt at humor and continued her story. "I thought and thought about what could have happened. Was church canceled? Were we meeting somewhere else? But then I looked across the street to the grocery store, which is closed on Sundays, and its parking lot was full. People were coming in and out as busily as you please. I didn't know what to think."

"If I was your age," I said, "I would have thought I'd died and ended up in a strange world."

Mom again ignored me.

"What I finally realized," Mom said, "was that the sun was sinking in the west, not rising in the east. I had only slept one hour, and it was still Saturday evening."

"So what did you do?" I asked.

"I went home and went to bed so I could get up at four to get ready for church," she replied.

Graffiti Artist

   As I watched an approaching truck, I recognized some artwork
on the side and smiled. I thought back to the first day of class a couple
years earlier when the students were introducing themselves. Wyatt's
introduction was unique.

   "I'm a graffiti artist," he said.

   "Not like the graffiti on buildings and trains, though, right?" I
asked.

   "Well," he said slowly, "yes and no."

   By this time the whole class was curious.

   "Would you like to expound on that, Wyatt?" I asked.

   "When I was a teenager," he said, "I started out painting train
cars with some friends. They got tired of it. But for me, there was an
adrenaline rush trying not to get caught. And I was good at it. I felt
proud when I drove by my art work and heard people say it was
awesome, even when they talked about how wrong it was for someone
to do it. And I hated not being able to tell them it was mine."

   "Did you ever get caught?" another student asked.

   Wyatt shook his head. "I came close a few times. One night
I'm sure the police knew they had me cornered, but they couldn't find
me. I stayed hidden all night. They stayed until the next morning but
finally left. It was winter, and I nearly froze to death."

   "Obviously something must have changed," I said, "or you
wouldn't be telling us this."

   Wyatt nodded. "I'd been doing graffiti for about four years
when I was out with a girl, and she asked me what I did. When I told
her I painted graffiti, she said that was awesome. As we talked, I
realized I didn't want to date someone who thinks it's awesome to

break the law. Then I realized I was the person breaking the law, and that was worse. I decided I needed to change.

"I went to my church leader and explained what I had been doing and that I wanted to change. The problem was, I had to admit that I loved doing it.

"'Do you love it because of the excitement of doing something wrong, or because it is a creative outlet?' the church leader asked me.

"I thought about it, and realized there was a little bit of excitement, but that was getting old. It was more the creativity.

"'Creativity is a part of human nature,' the church leader said. 'You need to take care of the illegal things you have done, but you also need to find another creative outlet.'"

Wyatt said he turned himself in and was sentenced to hours of community service, much of it scrubbing off graffiti or painting over it. But he couldn't find a creative outlet, and he could feel the desire to create growing within him. Then one day he heard a business owner talking to a customer.

"She said she needed to paint her shop," Wyatt said, "but she also said she wished she could get someone to paint a logo or picture or something instead of just a boring paint job."

Wyatt had an idea. By promising to repaint at his own expense if the owner didn't like his work, he talked her into letting him paint a graffiti-style logo on the building. The evening he started to paint, the police arrested him. The business owner had to explain their agreement before he was released. After that, Wyatt bought a suit to paint in so he looked professional. Graffiti art can take some getting used to, and at first, the owner wasn't sure she liked it. But she got so many compliments that she kept it and grew to love it.

Soon job offers poured in. Wyatt even painted cars, pickups, and trucks. He had a waiting list for months of work. He said he checked with the art department to see if it was possible to major in graffiti art. They had never considered it before, but Wyatt ended up making a good living at it while going to school.

As the truck whizzed by me, my thoughts returned to the present, and I smiled and said, "Nice work, Wyatt."

Date Night

When Samuel, a local church leader, arrived at the church for his weekly Tuesday evening meeting, he saw the usual group of cars pulling into the parking lot. They mainly carried teenagers and their leaders who were meeting for their weekly activities. But the Bishop also saw something he didn't expect. Walter was out mowing the church lawn.

Walter was almost ninety years old. He and his wife, Betty, had served in the community and the church all their lives. They had especially loved the youth. Though they had always wanted children of their own, they'd never been able to have any. So they seemed to adopt the youth of the community. Ma was a common nickname for Betty, and Walter was often called Pa.

Walter and Betty had always been asked to serve with the teenagers in their church. Either Betty was off with the girls camping, or Walter was hiking with the boys into the wilderness. Often the two of them organized fundraisers for youth activities. Together they had served the youth every Tuesday night and many other nights for as long as Samuel could remember. Even when they could no longer hike or camp, they still showed up on Tuesdays with ice cream or other treats.

But in the last year, Betty had become so sick that Walter spent every free minute he had taking care of her. Walter lovingly attended to every detail of Betty's care. Kind people had suggested that this was too much of a burden for someone his age, but he insisted that it was no burden at all. However, Walter had said that the thing they missed most was the Tuesday night activities. Samuel knew the teenagers missed Walter and Betty, too.

Then a couple of months ago, Betty had passed away. Walter was lost without her. His grief was so intense that everyone thought it would kill him. No one expected him to last long without her. He didn't come to church and was seldom seen outside his home. That's why Samuel was surprised to see Walter mowing the church lawns.

Samuel parked his car and walked over to Walter, who was busily walking back and forth behind the self-propelled mower.

"Walter," Samuel said, "what are you doing?"

"What?" Walter replied.

Walter was quite deaf, and the noise from the mower didn't help.

"What are you doing?" Samuel yelled.

Walter let go of the mower's throttle bar, and the mower went silent.

"I'm mowing the lawn," Walter replied.

Samuel nodded, feeling a little silly for asking an obvious question. "Yes, I can see that," he said. "But why?"

"Because it needs mowing," Walter replied.

Again Samuel felt sheepish at having asked an obvious question, but Walter wasn't catching the drift of the questions. "What I meant," Samuel said, "was, do you think you should be doing this now, at your age?"

"I'm not sure what age you think I should do it at," Walter replied. "And if I do it next week instead of now, I'll just be that much older."

"So why did you come to do it at all?" Samuel asked.

"The youth wanted to have a cookout here tonight," Walter replied. "And besides, it's date night."

"Date night?" Samuel asked.

Walter nodded. "Betty and I always made Tuesday our date night. We worked with the youth, and then we went out for a milkshake. I've really missed her, and I decided it was time for a date again." He paused and smiled. "I'm not sure, but I can almost feel her here with me right now."

Samuel only nodded, feeling too emotional to speak. And as the youth piled out of the church, many of them hugging Walter, Samuel felt Walter was right. Betty was probably there for her date with him.

A Scaredy-Cat

Our neighbors' dog, Rosie, didn't like cats. In fact, she wasn't too fond of many things. She had killed more than one batch of our kittens and at least a dozen of our chickens. She came snarling at us when we walked by, and I wasn't sure she wouldn't attack given a chance.

Our neighbors are good people and tried to keep their dog in. They installed an invisible fence, and that kept her home most of the time. But once in a while, there was something so fascinating that she would endure the shock to get out. Even if she didn't get out, she barked a lot. Often every dog in the neighborhood joined the chorus for the two a.m. bark. Our two dogs weren't immune from this devilish deed, and more than once I got up and yelled at them to be quiet.

But one night Rosie seemed to open the floodgates for a nightmarish bark fest. She went crazy with a bark I'd never heard before. Instead of a vicious "I'm going to kill you" kind of bark, it was an "I'm afraid for my life" one. My dogs joined in, seemingly calling out encouragement. Soon every light in the neighborhood clicked on as everyone shushed their dogs.

I soon had mine quietly whimpering, and so did almost everyone on the block. But Rosie kept up her racket even with her owners yelling at her. They were out in their backyard, and I know they were trying to take care of the situation. But Rosie barked for almost an hour. I finally had to close the window even though we had no air conditioning and the heat was stifling.

Eventually, Rosie stopped barking. I opened the window, but she was whining so loudly I had to shut it again. After a while, I tried once more, and all was quiet.

The next day I nonchalantly walked around the block, passing my neighbors' house, hoping to discover what had caused the problem. But there was nothing unusual except that Rosie didn't come snarling to the edge of the invisible fence line like she always had before. I knew she was still around because I caught glimpses of her, and I still heard her whimpers. But she didn't bark or act viciously.

A few days later I was out working in my garden, and the eleven-year-old girl from that family passed by on her bike. I waved at her, and she came over to visit.

"Did you hear Rosie barking like crazy the other night?" Melanie asked.

I nodded. "It was hard to miss. What happened?"

"My dad tried to piece things together from what he saw," she replied. "A young cat came into our yard with its head stuck in a glass bottle. Dad thinks Rosie attacked the cat because there was dog spit on the outside of the bottle."

"Did she kill it?" I asked.

Melanie shook her head. "The bottle was really thick, and she apparently couldn't bite through it. The cat kept running around backward in circles and was making an eerie noise as the sound came out of the bottle. Not being able to bite the cat's head, the eerie sound, and the cat's strange behavior apparently scared Rosie to death. Dad said he thinks Rosie thought it was a mutant cat that had come seeking revenge. She was at the farthest edge of the yard barking like she thought she was going to be killed."

"Yes," I said. "I heard that part. So what did your dad do?"

"He finally caught the cat, greased its neck, and set it free. It ran off, but Rosie kept whining, so we ended up letting her sleep in the house all night."

"I haven't seen much of her since then," I said.

"That's because any time a cat comes near our property, Rosie hides in her dog house and doesn't come out for hours," Melanie replied.

I smiled and thought that maybe I should walk our cat on a leash to protect me from Rosie.

The Tattoo

After church on Sunday, we loaded our harp into the van and connected the van to the tent trailer. We were soon on our way to a music camp for our daughter Elliana to be part of an orchestra and a choir. We arrived at our destination just in time to deliver our harp to one of the practice rooms. As Elliana took a minute to practice, the director told us about the camp.

"This is a premiere music camp," he said. "Students come from all over the western United States. Music people from all over the US come to help and to teach the students. Many of them volunteer and come at their own expense year after year."

Finished with the harp duty, we headed to the campground. Almost every one of the camp spots was full. We started visiting with the people there and learned that many of them were like us, there for their children to attend the music camp.

Even though we had the music camp in common, the diversity was greater than the commonality. Some parents were teachers like us, while others were wealthy businessmen. Some had tent trailers, and others had fifth-wheels and motorhomes worth a few hundred thousand dollars. There were people of different races and from all walks of life. Yet despite the differences, we all soon became friends.

I had to leave that evening to go home for a few days to work and to take care of commitments for our other daughter. When I went back to that music camp for the final concerts later in the week, Elliana had some fun stories to tell.

Her choir teacher was one of the volunteers. He was a big, burly man who wore short-sleeve shirts. At the curve of his right arm, where the shirt sleeve ended, part of a tattoo showed. At first, his size made everyone nervous, so no one dared ask him about it. But as time went on, the students in the choir realized he was just a big, fun-loving softie, and their fear of him faded away. One day he asked if anyone had any questions, and one of the students raised her hand.

"What is your tattoo?" the girl asked.

The choir director laughed and pulled up his sleeve. There on this big man's arm was a Disney tattoo. It had Mickey Mouse, Donald Duck, and many other Disney characters. The students laughed, having expected something more rugged.

"Why did you get that?" a boy asked.

The director smiled. "Well, I've always loved everything Disney. In fact, I've taken my choir to the competition there every year. We never did very well, always placing last or close to last. But one year I couldn't get my class to settle down and work. So I came up with this brilliant idea. I told them if they would work, and if we won the grand prize at Disneyland, I would get a Disney tattoo. I figured it was a safe bet since we'd never even come close to winning before.

"My students got in and worked, and we had a great year. I still didn't think we had a chance of winning since my school was small compared to the competition. But when we got to the competition, my small choir sang with such heart that they sounded like a choir twice their size. We ended up winning, and, well, that's why I have a Disney tattoo."

That night, as Elliana's director lead the choir in an incredible performance, I had to laugh at Mickey's head poking out to watch from the director's sleeve.

The Best Family

I used to be scoutmaster to eighteen boys. I'm not sure what happened in our community, but there were two sets of twins, and almost every child born at that time was a boy. They were great, though they weren't above trying to challenge me. I often found myself carrying two or even three packs up the mountain, and I never came down until I knew all the boys were safe.

I'm not the scoutmaster anymore, but I still love being with the young men. I'm getting older; I'm struggling more. We hiked five miles to Hidden Lake in the Jedediah Wilderness this year. It wasn't steep climbing like last year when we climbed Mount Borah, the highest mountain in Idaho. But we didn't camp on Mount Borah, so we only had to carry food and water.

This year my pack felt heavier than ever, but I still wasn't far behind the boys. I must admit I did carry some extra things. I was on a high adventure with the young men once when we took horses into the Tetons. The horses and food were all paid for. The outfitter obviously didn't know how much boys eat, and we spent a week being so hungry that bears didn't dare come near us for fear we would eat them. Since then I have always packed frozen bread dough and oil to make scones. This year was no exception. And when we settled down for dinner in the evening, the boys happily enjoyed the scones and honey butter.

As I shouldered my pack for the trip back out, it was much lighter, and the trip was mostly downhill. I was grateful because I was still so sore from the hike in that I could hardly walk. However, my muscles soon warmed up, and the soreness faded away.

As we walked, I enjoyed listening to the young men talk. It helped me know what was important in their lives. The boys talked about one family in our community who goes on a big vacation almost every year. Quite often this includes a cruise or travel to some exotic place that few of the boys have seen. The boys talked about the nice pickup that family had and how they traveled frequently.

One of the youngest boys, Jason, was quiet as the others talked. When we arrived at the trailhead, we put our packs into the vehicles and started to travel to another lake where we would spend the rest of the week. Jason was in my van, and as the other boys talked more about the one family, he finally said something.

"I wish I had been born into their family," he said. "They are so cool."

"What about your family?" I asked.

"My family isn't cool."

"Oh, really? Can't you think of any good things your family does?"

He was quiet for a minute, then shook his head.

"Let's start with the fact that your father is the scoutmaster, and he's up here driving the pickup with most of our gear and the canoes. And maybe your family doesn't go on cruises, but how many times have you been on horse trips into the backcountry of Yellowstone?"

Jason shrugged. "At least a couple of times every summer since I was five."

"There's not a person in your family that can't ride a horse, even down to your youngest sister," I said. "And think of all the fish you caught in Hidden Lake. Then you cleaned them, and we cooked them. You can build campfires, hike, camp, and do things other families only dream of. You've probably been to more backcountry lakes than most people will see in their lifetime. Every family is the coolest in some way. It's just that what we do becomes old and familiar to us, and we don't see it as new and exciting. Some in their family are probably saying they wish their family was half as cool as yours."

Jason thought about it a minute, then grinned. "My family is cooler than theirs, isn't it?"

I just smiled.

If you enjoyed this book, please a review on Amazon at:
http://amzn.com/1629860190

Would you like to see the *Life's Outtakes* column running in your local paper or magazine? Suggest it to the editor. If an editor runs the *Life's Outtakes* column due to your suggestion, we will send you a free autographed book by Daris Howard. Find out more at:
http://www.darishoward.com

Read stories, purchase books, or subscribe to our short story list by going to:
http://www.publishinginspiration.com

Daris Howard's Amazon page:
http://amzn.com/e/B004H76UGK

For inspiring plays and books, as well as discounts for booksellers, go to

http://www.publishinginspiration.com

About the Author

Daris Howard, an award winning author and playwright, grew up on an Idaho farm. He was a state champion athlete, competed in college athletics, and lived for a time in New York.

Daris has worked as a cowboy, a mechanic, in farming, and in the timber industry. He is now a college professor. He has also been a scoutmaster, having up to eighteen boys in his scout troop at a time. In his wide range of experience, he has associated with many colorful characters who form a basis for his writing. Daris has had plays translated into German and French, and his plays have been performed in many countries around the world. For many years, Daris has written the popular column *Life's Outtakes*, which consists of weekly short stories and is published in various newspapers and magazines in the US and Canada.

www.ingramcontent.com/pod-product-compliance
Lightning Source LLC
Chambersburg PA
CBHW071927220626
47052CB00002B/495